MADE IN THE IMAGE OF THE GODDESS

THE LEGACY OF ZYANTHIA BOOK ONE

CHANTELLE GRIFFIN

First published by Publicious Pty Ltd in 2013
Second edition 2017
by Chantelle Griffin

Interior layout by Chantelle Griffin
www.chantellegriffin.com

Cover artwork by Matthew K. Hoddy
www.spacepyrates.com

Catalogue-in-Publication details available
from the National Library of Australia

paperback ISBN: 978-0-9943921-0-7

Also available in ebook
ebook ISBN: 978-0-9943921-1-4

IN A WORLD OF SORCERY ONLY ONE WILL RISE

Saranon glanced up at the dragons as they flew overhead. The hour of darkness covered them as she watched on. She waited as Pennie examined the stone. It formed part of the shield locking them inside the camp. Shouts rang out on the other side. 'Is that Galven?' Pennie asked.

She nodded in reply. A twig broke on the muddy ground. 'We have company,' she said.

A lone sorcerer. Just one, but that was enough to give them away. Pennie ran for fear of being caught, while Tasha stood gazing out into the distance, 'One day that will be us.'

Enter an epic tale of sword and sorcery. More than two hundred years ago a powerful sorceress freed her people then vanished. As time passed truth turned into myth and myth became legend. The time has come again. Saranon must claim her rightful place before Zyanthia falls.

www.chantellegriffin.com

'I thoroughly enjoyed this novel, the fighting, the magic, the dragons it all came together in a wonderful introduction to this world and I am really looking forward to what comes next.'
Claire Ayres
www.brizzlelassbooks.com

For my sister

For all that has been before, for all the pain and sorrow, may you rise above them all. For the path less travelled brings hardship, adventure and triumph.

THE ZYANTHIAN REGION, TORDOREN

CHAPTER ONE

Rising from the ashes

The rubble caught between her fingers as Saranon peered down into the hole. It was not deep enough and the panic began to rise as Galven shouted from underground. She could not fail, or the time bought by the distraction would be lost. The cold wind swept through her tunic and she dug with her hands. It was no use the ground was too soft, from the rain that had fallen during the day. Tasha ran over, making no attempt to hide on the barren ground covering the low hillside. 'Get them out,' Tasha's voice was firm, 'Now!'

If she used her sorcery it would be detected in the camp and she would pay. Just as Galven and Jeremy had, for weeks they had been imprisoned in the sorcerer Keep.

It was by chance that Tasha found where they were. Saranon concentrated. The sweat cooled her skin in the wind that rustled through the trees in the distance. She held her hands out and willed her sorcery toward the hillside. Her palms ached as though they were on fire and the pain seared. Still nothing happened. Tasha watched in silence and then ran from sight. The guards sent up flares across the sky to signal the dragon riders. It lit up the darkness with a dim haze showing the desolate shabby buildings, that housed her and the rest of the Issola trapped in the camp.

It was all up to her. The cold air burned against her skin as she held onto her sorcery. Her eyes locked onto the direction of Galven's voice. She raised her arms and the ground ripped away. She fell backward into the undergrowth as the explosion hit its mark. The sodden earth disintegrated through the air leaving a heavy haze. She stayed low to the ground as the mud clung to her clothes. The cold soothed her hands as they ached. She glanced up as movement caught her eye. Tasha called out. The dull lights glowing through the camp were heading closer. Her heart thudded in her ears as she dashed the final distance. She skidded on the rough pebble surface behind the building.

She could just make out Galven and Jeremy in the shadows. If she stayed she would be found. Pennie signalled and she followed Tasha inside. She listened as the guards ran past the building. They fell silent as the guards shouted in frustration. Pennie peered through a slim hole between the wooden slats. Waiting until the guards had left. The sounds began to fade yet the lights remained. A great whoosh of air shook the building from overhead. Saranon glanced up through the small window. To see the underbelly of the dragon as it flew close to the ground. 'I want one,' she whispered in amazement.

Pennie snorted trying to muffle a laugh, 'You want trouble.'

'I can dream,' she said.

Tasha held her finger to her lips for silence. The cold night fell dark as the lights began to go out. There was nothing more they could do. She made her way to bed. She could feel the hard wooden crates through the thin straw mattress. She pulled the coarse wool blanket over her shoulders. Pennie fell asleep first, yet Saranon remained restless. Every time she closed her eyes she saw the image of her friends running in the shadows.

The walls of the building creaked in the wind, playing tricks with her mind. A man's voice spoke outside, 'Have you found them?'

'We'll flush them out tomorrow.' Lavena, the old sorceress that ran the camp answered.

It was a small comfort to know her friends had not been found. As her mind rested she fell asleep hoping they had made it.

Light shone through the small window trailing along the wooden floor, as the sun made its way over the hillside. The shadow of the sorcerer Keep Antavagon arched into view. The day broke warming the open room. She rummaged through the wooden crate, forming part of her bed. It was her turn to carry the small notebook and she wrapped it close to her chest using a ragged cloth. The bell swung as the guards made their way past. She pretended to get dressed amid the girls who scrambled before the door unlocked. The heavy chain from the guard's key hit against door and it swung open. They rushed passed before the staff fell across the last girl to leave.

Saranon winced knowing all too well what the pain felt like. Her bruises were a few days old. The agony of not being able to heal them without drawing attention was infuriating. The guard marched them across the worn pebble path to the old barn where they worked. The heavy crates were piled high near the main doors. Straw edged its way across the wooden boards. Cries rang out behind her and she fought the urge to turn. Pennie screamed as the staff came down on her, yet if Saranon turned she would be met with the same. A guard shouted, 'We found them.'

Lavena left and the doors shut behind them. Only then did she turn. Pennie was slumped near the wooden crates. Her arm outstretched, but her hand would not move. Saranon asked, 'Did she see?'

'No,' Pennie winced in pain fighting back tears.

Saranon looked back with a blank expressionless stare at Tasha. She placed her hand on Pennie's arm. If she flinched she would give it away. Pennie moved her fingers and Saranon walked away keeping her eyes on Tasha. The barn windows were high and long allowing the light to wash the space.

The footsteps from the guards at the other end marked the beginning of a long shift. She kept her head down and did her best to avoid attention. The notebook rubbed against her skin, but she dare not move it. She carried the full wooden crates across the open space between the wall and the bench. Some guards would let them eat the vegetables, but she could not chance it. She listened for every shout that rang out across the camp. She hoped that Galven and Jeremy made it. As the day blended into any other she began to lose hope, yet there was nothing she could do. They were on their own.

The toll of the bell for midday caught her off guard. She had been so intent on being busy that the morning had gone. The bright daylight shone as the three friends separated. Making their way to a stream that trickled through the camp. She picked up the coarse bread and ripped it with her teeth as she ran. Tasha stood close to the old tree overhanging the rocky bank. The sun shone golden across the ripples. The stream lapped against the pebbled edge. One day she would beat Tasha to their hiding place. She waited as Pennie scrambled through the bushes and doubled over catching her breath. She took care to remove the notebook and handed it to Tasha.

The stone markers were close. It was her duty to check the nearest one. She stepped along the rocks peering out of the earth. So she could avoid leaving a trace across the ground. There hidden in the scrub came the sickly glow. A faint green edge emanated around a stone almost as long as she. The sorcery continued without any hint of being broken. She reached out her hand wanting to touch it, but as she did a searing pain ran through her fingers. She held her hand there, determined not to admit defeat. It began to throb and she yanked it back. She made her way back as Pennie washed her face in the running water, winding down the stream. The other bank towered over them making a perfect hiding space away from the guards.

Tasha tapped the edge of the charcoal against the notebook as she gazed around. They gathered underneath the tree branches. Watching the sun glitter off the water as Tasha spoke, 'It will have to be soon.'

Saranon nodded. They had been planning their escape when Galven and Jeremy had been taken into the Keep. She had been there before, but the guards were on edge this time. Though none of them said it aloud they were the oldest group at the camp. No one knew what happened to the last ones to leave. It gave an uneasy feeling that made their escape all the more urgent.

The bell rang out cutting their time short and they made their way back through the scrub. Saranon took care to place the notebook back and wrapped it tight. She gave the cool water's edge one last look as the sun beamed down across the pebbles. She ran in line with the other girls piling into the straw covered barn. Gripping another wooden crate before anyone noticed her. The warmth from the spring air took the last chill out of the afternoon. By the time she had set the last wooden crate down, the pile of empty crates in the far corner stood as testament to the hard work. She wiped the sweat from her brow and took a breath of fresh air. The barn doors opened for nightfall.

Dinner was always late. It was a thin gloopy broth

that slipped off her spoon with the same consistency of water.

'Don't play with your food,' Pennie whispered.

She realised she had gazed at the spoon too long. Lavena was not looking and she breathed a sigh of relief. They washed up the wooden bowls before rushing into the building where they slept. The warm pebbles rubbed against her sore feet. She waited pretending to rest before Tasha tapped her on the shoulder. Pennie had already lifted the wooden slat. They squeezed through as the other girls slept.

Pennie had misjudged the guards. They hid close to the building waiting for the footsteps to pass. Her heart thudded in her ears as the steps grew louder. The guard was closing in on the corner of the building. Another guard spoke and the footsteps went away. They made their way along the pebble path in the dark staying together. The moon shone through the scrub, away from the buildings. They stayed close to the bushes hiding their shadows as they went. A magical glow fell over the stream at night and the wind rustled through the branches. Pennie unpacked a large handkerchief piled with food. She gasped at the sight, 'Where did you get that?'

'Shush,' Pennie said. 'You were so busy I thought you would need this.'

Her stomach rumbled in response.

As she ate Tasha spoke the words she had been dreading. 'I need you to break the stone.' A silence fell over the small group. 'I'm not able to do it and I know you can.'

She gazed down at the pebbles in the moon light as the stream lapped at her feet. Tasha was asking her to use sorcery, all that she could summon. She trusted Tasha, but it was a big task and she was unsure. 'Is there another way?'

Pennie waited before she spoke, 'I can check the connection again.'

It was all Saranon could ask. If she used her sorcery to try and break the stone it would summon all the Arthrose sorcerers in the camp.

They made their way through the scrub, along the rocks that broke through the surface. Pennie crept toward the stone marker as Saranon glanced around watching as she waited. The connection glimmered only for a moment and Pennie stopped. They hesitated, but only silence followed. Pennie began again, as the connection gave a dim light the wind rumbled with a whoosh. Lights flickered through the buildings in the camp. Saranon glanced up into the eyes of the first dragon as the riders flew overhead. For a moment their eyes met. She stared in defiance and the dragon flew past. The hour of darkness covered them as she watched on. She waited as Pennie examined the stone. It formed part of the shield locking them inside the camp.

Shouts rang out on the other side. The dragons flew toward the northern edge. A fireball of sorcery shot straight up lighting the night sky. 'Is that Galven?' Pennie asked.

She nodded in reply. A twig broke on the muddy ground. 'We have company,' she said.

A lone sorcerer. Just one, but that was enough to give them away and they all knew it. Tasha made the decision,

'Silence him.'

Saranon gave a curt nod and left running through the scrub. She circled in as the sorcerer tripped in the dark. He made a whimper as she braced her hands around his head. Her sorcery built up, it ran through without leaving a trace.

She stepped back as the sorcery flooded in. A voice called inside her head, but it was not her. She let go and the voice disappeared with it. Pennie almost ran into her, before heading straight back. The fear shone in Pennie's eyes and Saranon could not blame her.

Tasha stood for a moment and gazed out into the distance, 'One day that will be us.'

CHAPTER TWO

The end of the beginning

A pebble fell across the creek as the three friends hid, enjoying a brief moment as shouts rang out through the camp. The sounds brought with it the echoes of the only life Saranon had known. Her friend Tasha was not fazed by the possibility of being caught as they lay close to the edge of the shield. The stone marker shone bright within reach, but none of them dared touch it. The stone ward let off a sick glow visible through the scrub. Pennie had managed to scavenge the notebook that they hid, where no one would find it. Tasha now held it as her short pale wisps of brown hair glistened in the sun's rays, shining off the water's edge.

Saranon preferred not to keep notes, but Tasha insisted. Tasha made herself appear important with a serene stature that belied their predicament. Saranon listened although she tried not to show it. Her friends had been planning their escape, and as always it relied on her. She did not mind, it gave her a great sense of pride when her friends asked for help. 'Now,' Tasha spoke just above a whisper, 'I'm certain that a weakness in the shield lies here.'

Tasha pointed to a roughly drawn sketch, as Pennie eyed it with an unimpressed enthusiasm, 'So if you get it wrong we get fried.'

'What do you mean?' She asked Pennie and Tasha answered.

'No, if we time it right the worst that can happen would be a nasty shock,' then Tasha added 'and we would be stuck in the camp.'

'So nothing unusual then,' Saranon remarked, 'I'm in.'

They both looked at Pennie, who glared in a huff before finally giving in, 'Oh, all right.'

Saranon smiled there was something exciting about trying to escape. The thrill ignited her senses.

A sound carried too close to where they stood, and the small group scattered. Each made their way back to the main building from a different direction. Their meagre lunch break was over, as they scurried back to the hard work of the camp. Before she could dart in the building, the old hag hit out so hard across Saranon's back. She managed to stop herself from slamming into the ground. There were many reasons for wanting to leave the camp and no matter how much she tried to hide it, the thought glinted in her eyes. She made her way into the work shed, knowing it would be a long day before she could rest her weary head.

Long after the sun had left the sky, and the shadows had all but disappeared, Saranon made her way to bed. She longed for the day she could leave the camp. The thought filled her dreams with a never ending flow of images. All leading to one thought, escaping to freedom on the outside. She longed for the world as she imagined it, as the scenes filled the empty void with hope. It was a warm cosy thought that kept her snug, as she stayed in a deep sleep, resting her weary muscles for yet another hard day ahead.

The sky's murky grey clouds hung overhead, with an ominous gloom that wiped her dreams away. It filled the air below with a musty fog, gathering in a thick layer over the muddy grass which only added to the confusion in the camp. The old wretch in her fine clothes looked out of place, as she bundled Saranon up with the older children. They were taken into the depths of the mountain. Saranon had heard strange things whispered through the camp about what happened in the mountain. She went unquestioning as the other children did. A small group of rag tag tired and worn out youths. She knew Pennie and Tasha well, but that was all amongst the small group that huddled close together in the old coach. There was nothing to help cushion the ride as it jolted over a makeshift road. They travelled down into the deep darkness leading to nowhere.

The sky broke open with a great heavy rain, soaking the ground as the coach led the children inside. The large heavy doors shut behind them with a low groan that filled the air. The last of the sunlight slithered away out of the children's reach. They walked away in single file down the dirty well-worn steps. The sound of the droplets filled the silence, as they ran like sweaty perspiration down the chiselled outer walls. Saranon put her hand up to the wall, and it screamed at her. She flinched and snatched it back. The different screams filled her head and blocked her ears from the cries. Then she fell back down to reality as one of the caretakers shoved her back in line.

As they walked down the grimy steps they came to a large room where they split up and were taken further down. Her head filtered through the sounds she had heard. From somewhere through her pulsing heartbeat her mind put together the words, help me and she felt sick. The caretakers led her, Pennie and Tasha down to a room full of barred cells then pushed them in. The girls tried to get close to each other in the dim flittering light. This was not new for Saranon she had stayed like this before. When the caretakers had held her down, and marked her arm so that she would forever be recognised as an Issola.

She looked down on the mark on her arm, and wondered what she had done to deserve it. Tasha was trying to hold back tears, she hated the dark. Pennie put her arm through the bars to comfort her, as the two girls leaned on each other for support. As Saranon wondered what would happen this time, she rested her back against the wall. Her body felt limp as a faint presence entered her head and sifted through her thoughts as though she were not there. Her body fell forward and the contact broke as her head stung. Pennie and Tasha did not appear to notice.

As her hands fell forward she felt it crawling through her arms and down her hands.

Sweat poured down her cheeks from the pain, her hands felt so hot, she could not contain herself from screaming. The pain stung her eyes and she could feel herself go. Saranon woke up on the cold hard floor to find Pennie and Tasha staring at her, not knowing what to do. She could not move, her head hurt, and her nose had bled onto the ground. Everything seemed a world away as she tried to focus and as Saranon did she realised where she was. She laid her head back down on the grimy floor. Somehow a small ray of dull light had found its way through a tiny crack, to show that it was daytime outside. In the shock of sunlight creeping along the walls, the guards came to take Tasha away. The image did not register as her head still spun in a daze.

It was well into the night before Pennie reached over and tapped on her shoulder as she woke from her slumber. 'Can you feel it?' Pennie whispered.

'What?' she asked.

'I've been trying to find Tasha, but I can't sense her.' Pennie replied.

'Perhaps she wants to be alone,' Saranon knew she was only fooling herself.

'Please check,' Pennie always fretted when she could not sense one of her friends.

'All right, stop bugging me,' she replied.

The dark walls pulsed as Saranon gave in to the sensation, that she had been disciplined not to use, though luckily she had not let it get to her. She extended her energy, as she noticed it was easier to use and her reach appeared to be growing. It alarmed her, but there was no one here to talk to, except her friends who were none the wiser.

All she could do was accept whatever it was that expanded, and improved with every step that took her further away from what she had known. The bars faded into wavy red silhouettes through the expanding power of her mind. She did not notice Pennie as she stepped through the bars as though they were not there. The walls pulsated down like streams of flowing dark liquid with an almost rough feel on the skin. Yet she passed through with an ease that sent a shiver down her spine.

The floor seemed just a shadow of a memory underneath her feet as she pushed her hand against nothing. She stood up in the cool heat emanating outward and into the world. Saranon could no longer see Pennie, a sense of urgency swept over her, she had to find Pennie. She made out life forms of some of the guards that appeared in a faint form with a dull almost sickening dim glow. Up ahead she only just made out Pennie's light wavering form, it was far away. Saranon ran through the maze of forms ebbing through the shadows, but somehow that did not matter. She forgot Pennie for a moment and remembered her goal, to find Tasha.

It occurred to her that she had not sensed Tasha at all, as the worry inside her grew to an ever increasing panic. She had tracked Tasha down before this way, but this time something was different. Saranon's toes felt strange, she looked down, and her body seemed to be falling without the rush of gravity. A cold sensation thrust its way up her spine as she crumpled to a heap on the hard surface of the floor. The smell of blood came bursting thick and strong, hurting her lungs with a sickening dread.

As her sensations returned she could feel the taste of vomit in the back of her throat. Saranon's hand slipped on the wet floor and it was then that she looked up at the room. At the same time she stood her heart sank to the pit of her stomach. She realised there was no way out, she ran pounding her bloody fists on anything that looked like a way out. She could not cry, she did not want to, and Tasha would not have. Yet the tears blurred her vision as her breath caught up with her actions and she yelled out. She looked behind her and she knew that it could have, and should have been her.

The stench was overwhelming, yet she did not wipe the blood from her hands. Instead she went over and touched Tasha's forehead while wiping her own tears away. Saranon had to think and she could not. She knew deep down that this was her fate, and Pennie's. She realised she had lost track of Pennie. She leaned over the blood ridden patterns on the hardened surface of the floor. She could feel something calling her from far below, rising with a sense of urgency below Tasha's discarded body. It came closer, and closer, pulsing and rushing faster as it came. The walls started humming. Saranon had felt it before and she knew what it was. She leant over close to Tasha's face, 'This is for you. This is for us.'

Saranon reached out, and made contact with Antavagon. The great Keep had been dormant for so long, held back against his will, and now more than anything he wanted what was his. Without hesitation the central core hidden deep below embraced her. With it came the seething anger lying just out of reach. The great surge of energy from below rumbled through the building with a violent determination. It pulsated ever closer to her. This time Antavagon would have his revenge.

In the thrust of power flowing upward, she could no longer see Tasha's body. The Keep told her what she needed to know. Like a small silent rain, the tears were swept from their place on her cheeks, spiralling downward. Portions of the earth and the Keep appeared to rip free in the turmoil, sweeping her upward in a moment which seemed to take forever. She felt each hand grasp something solid and heavy, something not yet formed. The two swords formed through the air and the dust, her tears and the earth, two bond-breakers. The finest blades Antavagon could offer and he did so. In one small moment the Keep granted her the ability that so many longed for. Yet as Saranon held the blades she understood, strengthening her grip around them.

She held the most feared swords a sorcerer could use made of heart stone. The swords were a melding of the elements to form a solid material that resembled crystal, and sharp enough to cut through stone. The energy ran deep within and so did the thoughts of the Keep. As they filled her mind with an eager anticipation mixed with the darkness of dread. With the bond-breakers complete the sounds throughout the Keep rushed in and she remembered where she was. The sight of Tasha lay before her as a constant reminder as the Keep urged her on.

All too soon the swords were ready to use, Saranon ran her energy down the lengths of the Keep Antavagon. She knew what had to she had to do, what the Keep had called on her to do. With deadly accuracy the blades hit their mark; it was as though this was what she had been born to do. The guards had not yet registered the threat and fell quick underneath her, as she moved around with swiftness to her step. She could only just feel the bond-breakers; they were like extensions of her arms, doing her bidding. Too soon it was over, yet she knew it had just begun.

The power throbbed in her ears, as her eyes did not notice the real world. She became lost in the heat of her own energy, as it broke out in waves. She was able to make out Pennie and some of the children running away. There would be no one to run after them. The Keep whispered and she knew she had hesitated too long. The ground seemed to move and pulse in her wake as the memory of Tasha lay thick on her mind. She noticed her friend's blood still covering her hands, but that did not matter. What mattered now was clinging onto her power long enough to shut down the camp.

The guards were ready for her and the sorcerers held the dark sorcery close to their hearts. She could see and sense the taint as it wavered in the air. The dank smell was familiar to her now. Saranon's power washed over their fragile bodies, leaving nothing behind. They were no equal match for her. She had long suspected it, yet she had been too fearful to try. Saranon sensed the people, recognising other sorcerers that had been held in the camp. She could not understand why some of them were not leaving and it occurred to her they were still trapped. She pounded the earth so hard with her energy, that it ripped apart the buildings in its wake with such enthusiasm it frightened her.

This was no time to feel fear, as she remained calm and steady then moved on. As she found each tainted sorcerer her energy rippled inside her with a heightened enthusiasm as it wakened. The memories ignited by thoughts of Antavagon. She moved on bringing a path of destruction and the sorcerers ran, they all scattered in her path. As the buildings crumbled and the wards that had held so strong faded, the place became a shadow of what it once was. Now, it was Saranon's turn to answer, as her blows struck levelling the ground as she swept through what remained of the camp.

Saranon realised that the sensation she was feeling was satisfaction. A rough calmness settled inside as her breathing slowed. It was not what she had expected, yet the excitement still tingled within from a job well done. She soaked in the image around her as the smouldering shell of the building lay in tatters. She dreamed of this day, she had strived for so long to see an end, yet the meaning was hollow without Tasha. The memory of her friend held firm in her mind, and it darkened her thoughts. She had done this for Tasha, yet it was all too late.

Saranon stood surveying the camp she had just demolished. She had let go of the energy, and could feel its presence throbbing inside her, making it difficult to stand. The taste of vomit came back and she ran off to wash out her mouth at a nearby stream. The taste was foul, she realised she had not washed Tasha's blood off her hands, and spat the water out. As she washed her hands she washed away the last remnants of Tasha and the loss of her friend overwhelmed her. The Keep had told her what had happened, but it all seemed unreal and here she was for perhaps the first time in her life, unsure of what to do next.

'Saranon!' Galven shouted, 'Quick follow us, if you stay behind you'll be found.'

Galven was a sorcerer that Saranon had met from the first camp. He looked different, but she did not doubt his sincerity and followed at her own pace. Luckily she did not have to go far to see that Galven had reached help. Although riding on a giant black cat was not something she was able to contemplate in her current state. Out of the shock of it all she just accepted it as normal and hiked herself up behind one of the riders, a man with greying hair and a cold face.

As they left, Saranon saw that there were many other riders on misquew hidden near the river. As they took off and shot out into an open patch of field, this became clear. She had one of those moments, when she asked herself what she had done. For some reason her scrambled mind did not want to focus on any logical answer and she stayed in a state of bewilderment. She recognised a few of the other sorcerers, as her bond-breakers reformed themselves. The compact sized daggers sat one either side of her belt, looking as though they had always been there in two neat little pouches. One bond-breaker by her side had a crystal blade as clear as day and the other as murky as night.

Saranon's hearing faded in and out, she just managed to hang onto the man steering the giant cat. They came to a stop near a cluster of buildings part way up the mountain side. She almost fell as she came down. She was still trembling on her feet as Pennie rushed up and had to help her stand. 'I'm so glad you're here. You have to come and see the hall, it's so grand. I heard that the camps maybe closing forever, wouldn't that be great?'

Pennie was so excited that Saranon had not been able to get a word in as they entered the grand hall.

She had to admit it was quite breathtaking, but then she was still not feeling well. A sorcerer broke away from the side, and started walking toward her. He began talking to Saranon, 'You are not welcome here…'

Pennie turned around, and had a go at him, 'What do you mean? Saranon is one of us.'

Galven noticed what was going on and came over, 'Pennie is right.'

'Then you will explain where the bond-breakers came from.'

'The Keep gave them to me after Tasha died.'

'No!' Screamed Pennie and ran off holding back tears.

Galven explained, 'Keeps do not usually give bond-breakers to sorcerers.'

Saranon held out the bond-breakers for Galven, and he took them. 'They feel like they are yours, what do you think Max?' he handed the daggers to the man who had started all the fuss.

Max looked at the bond-breakers and then at Saranon. 'They are yours,' and gave them back before walking off.

'What happened to Tasha?' Galven asked.

'You don't want to know,' Saranon exclaimed.

Saranon found Pennie and together they consoled each other in the loss of their friend. More people were entering the hall, which filled her with hope that they would not have to go back. She could not stand the thought of going back. Pennie wanted to know what had happened, but she did not feel like talking. Her friend noticed a few familiar faces and with that Pennie was off. Leaving her to rest in a small make shift bed, one of many that were being set up. Galven came over, 'I talked to Max he's fine for you to stay, but he wants to talk to you later.'

'That's fine,' she replied.

'What happened?' he asked.

Saranon hesitated a moment then whispered, 'The Keep told me how to destroy the camp, and I did.'

Galven looked at her, 'But you couldn't have done all that Saranon.'

'I think I did.'

She followed Galven away from all the commotion that was going on. Along the way she noticed many faces, bewildered at the site of so many that had been held in the camp.

It was then that Saranon noticed something, 'I get the impression that you have been here for a while.'

Galven smiled, 'Yes. The Arroada managed to free me when I was moved from the first camp.'

'You could have told me,' she remarked.

'I thought you had enough to worry about.' He replied.

Galven took her to an area a little removed in the building, connected to the great hall by a narrow hallway.

The Arroada had a complex and advanced hospital the like of which she had not seen. The world felt dark and alien, closing in upon her as she let go of all the anxious thoughts that had clouded her mind in the camp. Galven did not appear to notice anything different, and she wondered how she could ever fit in. She was becoming her old self again. She could feel everything returning to normal as she took in the sounds and sensations of the small town on the side of Mount Eodarr. The sensations felt familiar as she reached out her hands and ran her fingers along the wall feeling the rhythm of the Keep. It spoke back to her vibrating through her fingertips, and sending words to her ears. She opened her eyes, and spoke the words that came to her mind, 'Aaron Wercaston.'

Galven looked at her a little unsettled. 'Galven, I would prefer to see Aaron alone,' Saranon spoke as she waited.

He nodded and with a stunned look Galven hurried away. Aaron was a greying well-built man who welcomed her inside the small room. Saranon sat down, she found the soft cushions and comfy bench rather unusual to sit on after the harshness of the camp.

Aaron smiled but looked concerned, 'What can I do for you?'

Tell him, whispered the Keep. Saranon did not know where to start. In the middle of all the confusion her mind was still hazy as she tried to think, so she began near the end. It was not easy letting go of something that would have cost her in the camp, something which cost Tasha her life. No amount of healing would wipe away the pain, and Saranon found herself crying. Aaron checked her over, 'You say that now you feel normal.'

'Yes,' answered Saranon.

Aaron stood up, and asked her to follow, leaving her in a small entryway while he left. She waited feeling like she was completely lost and annoyed, all at the same time. Aaron asked her to enter and she did, Max was there he spoke first, 'Saranon you have been given a great gift.'

'You mean a great curse,' Saranon said in a flat voice.

'We would like to find out the level of your sorcery,' Max asked.

She saw that Max was trying to be nice, but this did not suit his personality. He looked like someone who preferred to be outdoors and appeared to be uncomfortable in his surroundings. She went with Aaron to prepare, as he was explaining the process. It sounded quite simple, although she knew that did not always carry across to reality. Go into the room alone, relax and let her energy out so to speak. It sounded simple, but something told Saranon that this was going to be trouble, she had not figured out how. The Keep at Eodarr had gone quiet, not a good sign in her books which started to show through to feelings of agitation. 'Aaron, you are not telling me something,' she spoke.

Aaron laughed, 'I didn't say this would be easy.'

Saranon was beginning to wonder if she was up to this new challenge. Anything at the moment was better than what she had been through and she knew how to hold her own. The underground chamber smelt of dry acrid dust filtering through her lungs. She turned and Aaron had already shut her in. She was beginning to wonder if this was a mistake. She walked to the centre of the room and lay down as a small fog etched its way across the floor.

She thought its timing was too appropriate. She relaxed and was surprised to sense nothing that was not meant to happen. It would not be the first time she had been tricked. She thought that at least she should give the process a try before giving up. She still felt nothing, and could not understand what was going on. She got to her feet, and shouted, 'This isn't funny!'

Saranon turned around to try and open the door, only to be confronted with a smooth surface containing no remnant of an opening.

She pushed out with her energy so harsh it almost ripped at her skin, and felt like fire. She screamed, and could not see through her swollen stinging eyes. How could they? She thought this was nothing but a trick. She called through her mind and thought so loud she called to the

Keep. Saranon drew the sorcery up to her, and her down to it. She reached as far down as she could and yanked the energy so hard she thought she was going to break.

Saranon wanted to scream, but could not. It hurt to breathe and somehow through everything, she saw what she was looking for. She reached out, and touched it with both hands. She hit the solid ground with harsh thud that brought her back to reality. The floor of the chamber was ice cold and her hands were shaking as she tried to get up. There were voices behind her as the door to the chamber burst open, with a great boom as the vacuum ended. With help Aaron picked her up, and laid her down on a stretcher to take her away, through an array of muddled hallways. 'It's all right, it's over,' he told her in a voice that was far too calm.

CHAPTER THREE

Following the original path

It would be Pennie's fifteenth birthday soon. Her friend was a few months younger and had insisted that Saranon have a late birthday to join in the celebration. She was becoming aware that her friend had not come out of their ordeal as well as she had. Every now and then she would catch Pennie staring off into space, as solid and pale as a statue. It reinforced her view that if something was going to happen it was up to her to sort out. 'Get up!' Pennie shouted.

The light of the morning shone through the window, and into her eyes. 'You have to open your present,' Pennie was sitting on her bed.

It occurred to her that she had nothing for Pennie. So she reached over, and took hold of the crystal clear bond-breaker Attourin she had made earlier, then passed it to her friend. 'I want you to accept this.'

Pennie was so ecstatic she hugged Saranon, and ran off to tell everyone who was awake or soon would be with all the commotion. She stared down at the palms of her hands nothing could wash away the imprint of Mount Eodarr, the mark of sorcery. She kept the marks covered from sight, they felt cold. One a murky red and black, and the other on her right hand a mix of white and blue, with a smooth finish where the skin of her palms should have been. It had frightened Max to see them, but nothing seemed to astonish her. It was part of her hands and part of her. She did not see what all the fuss was about.

Her birthday morning seemed unusual with all the activity around the place. The air smelled sweeter as the sunlight warmed the room. She finished putting her jacket on and caught a glimpse of Mira's elegant long dress as the older sorceress swept by. Mira was a middle-aged lady who had kept her beauty well, though her greying hair betrayed her real age. She followed and Mira turned. There was something wrong. Saranon could sense it from the people around her. It was like a stale smell wafting through, spoiling the air that had only just reached her.

The sensation was strange, 'Have we been found?' She asked.

Mira smiled, 'No, you are safe here.'

Mira was one of the great Council members for the Arroada. The older sorceress had shown great wisdom which Saranon respected. Mira had managed to win support for closing the remaining detention camps scattered in the north. The older sorceress seemed to understand her friend Pennie. That took a weight off her shoulders, 'Are you coming to the party?'

'I would not miss it,' Mira replied.

With that she ran off forgetting her concerns, and went to help Pennie get ready for the event in the evening. The world was just how she had imagined it, and Saranon had not felt so relaxed for a long time. She wondered how such a short time could feel so great and feared that it would end. She had become impatient about waiting for her hair to grow, so she had made her brown hair long with her sorcery. It flowed down past her shoulders much to her satisfaction. With Pennie making sure the hall looked perfect the day soon faded away, while her friend had no problem meeting the guests. Through the excitement something caught her eye. Mira and Max were talking with a group of people. They looked her way, then Max walked off.

Before she had a chance to do anything else Pennie grabbed her hand. Her friend hauled her through the crowd so fast she almost knocked Galven's friend over. It was hard not to join in the dancing and soon she lost track of time. In the morning Saranon grew suspicious, something was going on. The sensation tingled at the edge of her senses annoying her even more. She would have preferred to know what was happening. She did not have much luck in that area and figured she would have to rely on herself to find out.

She had not been able to keep her thoughts from

Pennie, who declared that she was going to find out what was going on before Saranon did. In the clear open air of Felgrai she found time to leave the quaint little town in the edge of the forest and travel alone. Her curiosity had gotten to her so much that she would sneak out in the night. Max did not appear to suspect that she was travelling alone. With Pennie's help and listening to passers by she had managed to find a few places the public would be welcome to listen to what was going on.

The first time Saranon went into a gallery to listen to the politics, she found herself going with a sorceress by the name of Tina. Pennie had no trouble striking up a conversation. Without discussing too much she found that all three had something in common. She was so nervous. This acted to confirm to anyone who saw her, that she was a sorceress of no such importance and not worth paying much attention. The great hall of the Arthrose Council stood in a grand elegance that took her breath away as she entered. The delicate carvings, marble and gold were in stark contrast to anything she had seen at the camp.

She noticed that she was not the only one looking up at the ceiling and at the paintings on the wall. Taking the whole scenery in as she gazed about the grand room. It was so draining having to sit still through the meeting. She looked over, and noticed that Tina did not seem to have any trouble at all. There had been a few moments where she clenched the seat so hard from trying not to let her anger out. Saranon thought that no one had noticed. The sorcerer keeping order over the meeting had looked her way more than once.

She left the meeting with a firm realisation that they would continue to be a problem for the survivors of the camps. More worrying was the air of agreement that hung around the gallery with a sickening dread that ate away her hopes. The Arthrose Council appeared to have support. She clenched her fist, holding back a rage of thoughts as they spun through her mind. She did not understand, it seemed absurd that the camps would have support. She did not like to contemplate the thought, as her hope mixed with an edge of sadness. This was not what she had expected to find in the real world, in her dreams it had all been so easy after escaping the camp.

Saranon stood, and left the chamber. The night air was sharp and cold as she said goodbye to Tina. It was a long journey home from Dreggan. On the outskirts of the city the stars made out the path ahead shining on the buildings.

She came across the conversation of two sorcerers walking by.

'The sooner the Arroada are dealt with the better.'

'Don't worry, Aimen has sent a group down.'

The masculine voices faded with the shadows that had carried them. Her paranoia had not been for nothing as her heart pounded heavy in her chest.

The only thing she could think of doing was to warn the Arroada, she did not know the place well enough to trust anyone else. She ran to where her misquew was who had been dozing off, concealed from the surrounding world. She almost tripped as she heaved herself up. This was no time to be complacent as she masked her entrance through the lay-line, it would take time for her to return. Saranon made it as far as an outer post and rode past the agitated guards. No one here would be pleased to see her.

She managed to locate Jeremy, Galven's friend. He came out to greet her 'What are you doing here?'

'I went to Dreggan, and I overheard that the Arroada will be attacked. Can you warn them?'

The sorcerer nodded as he relayed the message. Saranon had no intention of making Jeremy's life difficult, as she sat listening to the gentle hum of the small Keep. Words formed in her mind, the Keep was already letting the Arroada know, but would it be too late. She stood up as Jeremy came back, he exclaimed. 'It is not safe for you to return, you can stay here.'

She did not like being in the dark. She wanted to stay as Jeremy had told her, but something felt wrong. She poured her energy out along the ground, the sensation came back thick and strong; the Arthrose. Her anger swelled from deep inside her, suppressed for so long, when she thought that she could do nothing to stop them. This time it would be different. Saranon left the fort, with Jeremy calling after her to stay. Whatever sorcery they were using to try and make her stay, it was not enough. She ran through the security shield that held around the building with no hesitation, or halt in her stride. Her misquew was waiting for her on the edge of the small Keep and she leaped onto the lay-line that would lead her to one place.

Her veins pulsed with the quickening speed. She felt cold, but somehow more alive knowing now that she had a purpose. The building ahead looked calm as she approached in the cool night air. The Keep lay almost serene as she strode toward and she wondered if it had always been like that. Saranon shook that thought away, the Keep did not notice she was there, if it had it was not giving her away. She entered the building, where would the Arthrose be? She stretched out her mind. In that moment she had been noticed, she had to act racing up to the main tower. The security seals were stronger and for a moment she doubted herself.

Her determination kept her going as she hid in the shadows waiting for the footsteps to fade in the distance. She did not make a sound as the thrill of the chase circled around in her mind. She knew she had to take care, if she moved with haste the moment would be gone. Then it would all be for nothing and she was not prepared to give in. Just as she thought it was too late, a noise emanated from the other rooms, as a mix of emotions carried through a wave of relief. Yet all this was short lived as she held onto a single thought. She had lost too much, it had all been too much, and now she would have her moment.

Saranon could sense a commotion rise as it rattled her nerves and she blocked the thought from her mind. She had to focus, she was near her goal and yet so far, all at the same time. She took a deep breath steadying herself as she let the energy rise. Seeping through like an eternal tide crushing the last of her fading nerves. Yet at the same time it stirred something from deep within, an unknown panic that she tried to subdue. The Keep stayed silent, it had no business here, as she expanded her senses through the wall and beyond.

As her head thudded with the pulsing energy she rose, this time it would be different, this time it would end. She threw her sorcery in a wild rage shattering the bulky door, as the seals broke spraying the burnt smell of ash in a cloudy haze. Saranon did not falter, her mind stayed on one thought and if she did not succeed she would lose more than Tasha. She managed to hold back her underlying rage as it seethed just below the surface. She moved forward with a blind stubbornness that drove her on.

The first blow came from the right as she blundered through the door, but the pain seemed irrelevant, it was a common friend. Their faces seemed to blur as she interrupted the councillors of the Arthrose. She had entered their most sacred place and for that she did not expect to live, but then this was not about living this was retribution. As her wild rage crept to the surface, the energy poured out demanding release. The blast struck in a curved arc that lit up the room as it seared through the air, while the sorcerers blocked as the tension showed.

Saranon could hear a muffled voice yelling to get something and for a moment silence pounded through the air. This was it, the only thing holding her back was she. She looked up at all the sorcerers around her and saw them in such clarity she could see the beads of sweat on their faces. The air buzzed around her, yet the image was crystal clear as her energy pulsed in her ears, muffling the noise. She was trapped in a moment as it slowed to a steady grace and she lashed out with her energy as they answered in return. On the edge of her vision a ripple blocked her focus and caught her attention.

An aging sorcerer began to approach with something hidden under his robe, and then she saw it. The Eye of Escora legendary Orb of Darkonia and made by Zeralden Hadenvar. The Orb shone with a murky glow absorbing the light from the air, as it pulsed with a radiant heat sweeping across the room. She felt herself falling into a trance that beckoned to her being from the edge of the darkness. The strength of the Orb pulled at her senses like a tight vacuum, Saranon tried to resist, but it would not let go. She thrust out her energy against it, yet the Eye of Escora absorbed the blows.

She could hear the voices around her fade as she realised the Orb was stripping her sorcery away and she winced. It should have hurt, yet she felt no pain. The Orb called, and she threw all the energy she had toward it. There was nothing left as the void filled her mind and an energy from deep within engulfed her in a raging flood, as it burst to the surface. She remembered to breathe as a gasp fell across the room in the silence. In the faint glowing light she stood, as the sorcery of old that lay within called to the Orb, and it answered in return.

For the Eye of Escora had been made for a purpose, one that Saranon was yet to understand. It called out to her as the faint glow intensified filling the room, and the noise around cascaded toward her ears. The pain creased in through the edges, yet it did not matter. As she stood she could see the wave of shock, as a recognition swept through the sorcerers. This time she had the Orb. She breathed as the dust settled, the Eye of Escora held tight in her grasp. The library at Felgrai had come in useful, there would be no more kneeling as she stood up and let go to the energy within.

The Eye of Escora was hers, as she held it in both hands the Orb glowed with a certainty she did not have. Yet the energy within pulsed strong as she let it flow into the Orb, it grew brighter with a wild radiance. Before she could do anything more the Orb boiled with a raging heat, the pain seared through, and she had to let go. As soon as she did, she knew it was a mistake. The explosion from the severed link to the Eye of Escora shattered through the room with a thunderous spray. For a moment blocked out any noise, as the ringing filled her ears.

She felt numb as she opened her eyes, and the haze cleared. The smell of ash lay thick in the air, as she wondered how she had managed to escape the full blast. The Orb was cool to the touch and dark as she held it in amazement, not wanting to let go. The sound returned to the room as her head spun, and she almost dropped the Orb. The deadening blast had blackened the edges of the room as she looked on in disbelief.

For a moment Saranon thought the only thing the Orb had damaged was the building. Then she came back down to earth, and the pain began searing up her arms. The place was a mess with the charred outlines the only remnants of the Arthrose, she coughed remembering to breathe. Stammering past the charred table she slipped on the paper scattered over the floor. She could sense movement heading in her direction, as she noticed the papers in front of her. The documents held details of people sent to the camps and she leant down as she felt sick. One paper near her hand had come loose from its folder. She pulled it all the way out, and saw Princess Antobathia's name on it. She shoved it in her pocket, and ran as the shouting came close behind her. It felt like she was on her last ounce of energy and her ribs ached as she ran.

The sounds grew closer and the panic as she moved with her heart thudding in her ears. She held the Eye of Escora not wanting to let go as she ran from the Keep, darting out into the cool night air. The breeze swept across her face as the sweat poured down her cheek and yet she carried on not wanting to look back. Even though the sounds had faded well into the background, she could still sense the sorcerers. They were in the distance searching as they drew closer. Saranon finally stopped, catching her breath as her lungs ached. She was overcome with exhaustion, but she had to go on. Near the outskirts of the town she could sense movement as a misquew raised its sleepy head. Its eyes shone bright as soon as it spotted her.

Without any hesitation she ran towards it as the air hurt her lungs with every breath. She sat on the misquew and raced onto the nearest lay-line which led east to Ollanthia one of the oldest Keeps from the days of

Zyanthia. If there was a time she needed refuge, it would be now. As the misquew moved, a pain ran up through her side and across her chest, she gazed down to the wound as the pain crept in. Saranon stopped the bleeding, but she knew it was not good. She began to think the only reason why she had found it easy to leave, was because no one thought she would be alive.

She groaned with a hint of annoyance at someone thinking she had passed away when she was alive, yet the thought had an appeal to it. If it meant that no one was chasing her she could relax and she was in no state to fight even with the Orb. The wound was sucking away the last of her strength as her hands became numb while trying to hold on. The misquew was giving her no comfort when it jostled around as it moved forward. The riding cat sprinted at a low pace, just enough for Saranon to hold on. Her eyes grew tired as the death of her friend Tasha plagued her thoughts, like a recurring nightmare that would not leave her alone.

The image haunted her still as she moved through the night, it made the victory bittersweet and she wondered if it was all for nothing. The lay-line faded way as she reached the end. Without any warning the misquew dropped her down, then vanished into the darkness. Before her stood a powerful Keep, even in the night its brilliance shone with the glow stemming from within. She forgot how tired she was as she made her way forward at a heavy pace. The feeling in her side was beginning to numb and she felt weak as she managed to move on.

Ollanthia was beautiful with its monumental well-kept gardens. It was like a small piece of paradise that even the most powerful people were too superstitious to disturb. Sweat poured down her back soaking into the blood on her clothes. She had been lucky, if it were not for the Eye of Escora tucked close to her side, she was sure she would be dead by now. The enormity of what she had done hit her and the tears ran down her face, glistening with the glow from the moon light and Ollanthia. She had to tell Pennie, her best friend would not be impressed.

Saranon steadied herself as she neared the outer gate, it was late and the guards did not like wanderers at night. Gus, an old stocky man she had met before saw her first; 'What've you done?'

Gus placed his hand on her shoulder and helped her as she almost lost her balance. He muttered, 'We'll get you inside.'

His arms were like stone, holding her up as they walked along. She was lifted onto a make shift bed as the surgeon started peeling away the cloth to examine the wound.

Saranon woke up later in the ward with an aching pain, Gus was sitting beside her. 'You were lucky,' he said in a stern low voice.

He looked tired and shaken, and she guessed that he stayed up the whole night. She had a dull ache, but told Gus that she was all right. She did not have the nerve to worry him more than she already had. The light streamed in bringing its warmth through the window with the morning light. The Keep began to come alive with the daily activities.

Saranon noticed the people walking past looked nervous. Then she thought it would not take long for the news to reach the whole of Darkonia. She hoped they had not guessed, but then it occurred to her that the Eye of Escora was with her, anyone who found it would know. Gus saw the panic on her face and pointed to her belongs underneath the chair, on the other side of the bed. She had to figure out how she was going to leave. A sharp pain pierced her body from her quick movement and Saranon realised she would not be able to go anywhere. Gus stretched out of his cosy spot in the armchair, and said his goodbyes as he headed off for a well-earned sleep. This was not what she had expected. Although the thought had crossed her mind, her situation could have been much worse.

CHAPTER FOUR

A promise to a friend

Saranon hit the pond's surface with a small flat stone and watched as it skimmed across the still dark water at a mighty speed. It was hard not to lose her temper with the Guardians of Ollanthia for running off with the Eye of Escora for safe keeping. She felt trapped and that was not a good place to be for anyone on the receiving end of her frustration. Pennie was due to arrive soon, after almost going off at John the Head Priest. The others had not known how to calm her. So here she was cooling down. She had been cooling down for the last few days after getting out of the uncomfortable hospital bed. The only surprise was that some of the residences began to look upon her with fear, not that there was anything scary about her.

She lay down on the grass calming her thoughts and lying still, as she sensed the Keep spreading down deep underneath the ground. It made a soothing sound, but that was not what she wanted to find, and she heard a sudden burst of laughter in her mind. Was the Keep laughing at her? She could not tell. Saranon heard a sound behind her that broke her concentration. The mirage that had been part of the hill had faded away as the Keep opened one of the passages into its murky depths. The door sounded like it had not opened for quite some time. Grime had built up around the edges, but the air inside was still fresh. The room appeared like a large foyer with stairs leading in many directions and she took the ones to the right going down.

If Saranon was not able to have the Eye of Escora she was going to find out more about Ollanthia. Her annoyance at being treated like an ignorant child faded as she slid deeper down. She thought she could communicate with Keeps better than people. At least Keeps were simple and easy to work out. The tunnels led down to the primary systems and the central core. The system transferred energy from far below the ground into the core and turned into a usable energy source. Most central cores were located deep in the ground where the temperature was warm, and this one was over a thousand years old.

The air was growing warm. Brushing along the skin on Saranon's arms it was a friendly welcoming sensation. She could sense the Keep, it almost wanted her to continue, as though it was excited to meet her. She continued her downward path. As the tunnels became larger and more elaborate with details carved into the walls. She ran her hand along the patterns. The Keep sang in her mind and she let it guide her way as some of the patterns lit up showing the way ahead.

The tunnel was deep, falling away into the ground, as she almost slipped on the wet moss creeping out from the corners of the stairs. All Saranon could think about was what she had done, something inside her knew she would have to leave Darkonia. There were few places to hide from the Arthrose. The tunnel led into an underground atrium with the light from the markings mimicking the light from outside. The Keep knew where it wanted her to go and led her into a makeshift storeroom. She ran her finger along the dust, the object underneath glowed transferring warmth to her cold hands. This was what the Keep had brought her here to find. The markings on the walls shimmered, and Saranon ran back up the winding staircase taking two steps at a time. The light rippled through the glowing marks like an imaginary soft breeze leading to the outside.

It was dark, she was sure she could not have spent that much time inside the Keep? John was waiting off to the side with several Guardians of Ollanthia. He looked half stunned to see her, but she did not seem to notice. All she saw was a group of priests that were starting to close in on her. If Gus had not told her that they were peaceful, she would have thought they were being hostile. John spoke, 'I do not know what the Keep sees in you. Your actions pose a threat to Darkonia we will find you safe passage to Alveron, after that you are no concern of ours.'

The words took her by surprise they were not as friendly as she had been lead to believe. Then she had not thought through what would happen afterward. The priests huddled together as they left her out in the open and once again Saranon felt the isolation press against her soul. How could she do this by herself? How could Tasha leave it all up to her? Tasha had always been the one whose faith in the future had been unwavering. Here she was wondering if anyone else would understand. Later she cried herself to sleep.

She was about to rush off to work on the project Ollanthia had given her when Gus interrupted. Pennie peeped around the door to the lounge room. She burst in with her head held high full of excitement. She lightened up the room as Gus disappeared down the corridor in amongst the exchange of greetings. 'Do you have any idea what you've done?' Pennie said, 'The Arthrose is in such a mess.'

'I thought you would be angry.'

'Saranon,' Pennie went calm, 'It appears that I was infected with a virus at the camp. So what do I care about the Arthrose.'

A tear escaped down Pennie's cheek as she sat quietly in the armchair, 'I know you have to leave, the authorities are not sure how to deal with you. If they figure out it was luck they will be here in an instant.'

Her friend looked so much younger than her, so small and fragile. To get so far and be told 'Sorry you do not get to enjoy life, that is for someone else' was cruel. Saranon knew that her health was okay and she could not help but feel guilty that she was not in the same situation. She took

Pennie to see what she had been working on, far below the ground away from the outside world. Just for a moment, they could be children again.

Pennie decided her mission was to help get her out of Darkonia and frequently left the Keep. Her friend had told her that there were people watching Ollanthia to see if she would leave, or to make sure she was still there. After all if Saranon could kill the Arthrose Councillors, what else was she going to do? Some of the people could be seen from the gardens. Gus always looked as though he could tell exactly where they were and had pointed a few out. For some reason she had difficulty picking them out, but it did not worry her. She was too intent on finishing the project that had begun, to resemble a bond-breaker, in the form of an elegant sword.

Perhaps Ollanthia knew what was waiting in the wings, after all it had seen a few battles in its prime. Although she had grown up in the camps she had not been in a position to fight back. It was a new sensation that made her feel as though she had control. She stood back admiring the finishing touches on her creation. She blew across the surface of the blade and the air sparkled. The hilt was just as fine, light weight and manoeuvrable. She held the sword and it made a small whistling sound as the blade cut through the air. A large dull sound whipped down the walls of the Keep and tingled down her spine. It took a moment for Saranon to realise the Keep was warning her.

She fled upward, and almost ran straight into the new comers. She rushed into another stairwell then everything went quiet. She could not understand why she was having trouble sensing them. The Keep told her someone was approaching. Saranon realised she would have to go back down, and try to get out another way. She changed direction, rushing as she fled toward a short cut. As the door was closing she caught sight of a dark clad man wearing the symbol of the Royal Darkonian Army, then the room went white in a flash. Somehow the Keep managed to close the door and down she went with the flash still in her eyes. She realised she was crouching and stood up. Her head turned to the great chunk that had been torn out of the wall behind. As her vision cleared she could make out one of the attackers through the damaged wall and ran.

The echoes of the wizardry blasting through the rest of the wall followed her as she went. The sound sending shivers down her spine as she quickened her pace. She still could not sense them as she made her way to the outer rim of the Keep. Her heart thudded heavy in her chest as the shouting drew near. The sinking feeling hit her stomach as she realised she was not going to make it. She turned around; she had to find another way.

John had been right it was too dangerous to stay in Darkonia. As Saranon stepped through, the door disappeared back into the wall. There were a few paths that led in the direction she wanted to go, but from now on she would have to be prepared. She started heading north and sensed something familiar the Eye of Escora. She turned and plunged the sword through the seal on the door. The blade slid through with ease. As she entered the Orb was in open view in the centre of the room, she was about to rush in, and the Keep stopped her.

There were shields surrounding the Orb, this was not the first time she had encountered such devices. She calmed her mind, relaxed her body and moved forward. The shields sensed stress, anxiety, and extreme emotions. As much as she tried the explosion had scattered her thoughts, and she took a deep breath. For days with the bond-breaker she had been practicing a heightened level of concentration, it paid off as she reached the Orb. Now she was left with the difficult bit going back and she let out a small sigh. She knew her concentration had started to waver. The ripple of the walls as she went through felt heavy and made her queasy. Her stomach muscles flexed as she passed through the last shield. She bent over before emptying the remains of her dinner on the floor.

Saranon hurried through as the door closed, she had to go up. No doubt that would be expected as she thought of the blast. She had to approach the task with care. These were people who wanted her out of the way. She held no grudge against the Darkonian Army, but if they were involved she would have to be strong. She did not know much about them, or their capabilities. Her palms were already sweating and she was still feeling sick. She heard noises and braced herself one last time before opening the door to the next level. The energy rose up inside her and out stepped Saranon.

She held the blade Tellembre as it swung with ease, glowing hot at the hilt. The mark of the old crest rested on the shoulders of her robes. The room was a blur with the only way out through the people that stood in her way. Before the blade met them there was a momentary look of horror. As she blasted a way through, hoping she would not have to use the bond-breaker. As the wizards regrouped she ran toward the exit, yet just as she cleared the last gap a blade swung out to meet her head on.

She held up Tellembre as her blade sunk through without hesitation. She flung herself over the scattered mess, with a momentary glance back. Her heart seemed to be pounding from somewhere else, yet on the outside her appearance was almost serene. The bond-breaker moved with ease in her hands. Saranon's next encounter ahead had heard the commotion hesitating in her wake. They seemed to blend into the background letting her pass as she moved onward and north to the outer perimeter of the Keep.

As she ran through a large foyer with several corridors tailoring off, a stench became heavy in the air. Saranon knew what it was, she recognised the sorcery from the camps. This time it would be different, she poised herself ready for the embrace. Her lungs filling with the heated air as the coils spun around, this time would be different indeed. The coils became tighter and she laughed on the inside. She had been waiting for this, as they pulled tighter pinning her arms close.

In the fraction between her heart beat she exhaled and the six sorcerers came in closer to strengthen the coil. Saranon's heart beat and the sound reverberated smashing the sorcerers' strands. That flicked back, spraying the harsh light all over the room. The shock of the rebound took out the sorcerers, leaving nothing but charred marks up the walls. She gasped yet she could not let the shock sink in, she was so close to the edge of the Keep. As she made her way through the courtyard, there was no sign of the trouble within.

Compared to that, the rest of the way was easy. She cleared the perimeter on her misquew, riding a long distance before slowing down. Her brow was sweating and her arms felt heavy with exhaustion, it was all she could do to stand up straight. She hoped the focus had been on Ollanthia, as Saranon did not want to run into trouble. She held up her talik, a small round disc that could open small enough to fit in the palm of her hand. She placed her thumb on the centre of the outside, it had picked up a signal from Pennie which she answered and then waited.

She started to shiver as her back grew cold from the sweat, she could see her own breath in the cool night air. The river running past refreshed her face as she bent down. The sound of Pennie's misquew came from behind. It was a moment before she realised it was not her friend she had sensed. Saranon stood up to find a wizard dressed in the robes of the Darkonian Army. She was too shocked to speak as they seemed to be appearing from everywhere. Jacob stared down at her with a calm composure, 'You have no place in Darkonia. You have two choices leave, or stay and die. Which one will it be?'

She held back her rage, how dare he trick her and he had used her friend to get to her.

She stepped closer, the soldiers had surrounded her but kept their distance. It was definitely a trap. 'If you cannot send your own message, do not use my friend. I am not staying now get out of my way.'

Jacob reached out, and held onto Saranon's shoulders, 'You have a lot to learn.'

She went limp in his arms.

Noise came to Saranon's ears first.

'What do you mean you couldn't restrain her?' Major Shenoff was seething.

Captain Jacob Assinden spoke with a calm tone 'It disintegrated. I would not have believed it had I not been there.'

'So you brought an Issola here and we have no means of controlling her.'

'The Arroada are certain she is not Issola.'

'What would they know? Saranon is your responsibility, if anything happens it's on your head. I don't want to see you until she is gone the Alveronians can deal with her.'

Saranon found herself in a large room, a fire warmed the air. The soldiers were intent on playing cards nearby. She thought she saw Pennie, but it could not be, why would she be here? Pennie leaned over, and touched her old friend's head to reassure her. She whispered, 'I'm sorry about what happened, I couldn't think how to get you out otherwise.'

Her mouth tasted like vomit and she realised she was thirsty. She sat up in a rush and scared one of the soldiers. An older one laughed and told him to sit down. The older one Roger introduced himself and gave Saranon a glass of water, 'That's some bond-breaker you made.'

She realised the bond-breaker was missing and Pennie told her she had stored it in a safe place. Her head pounded, she was not happy about her friend's way of helping, though Pennie had not let her down. So Saranon resigned herself to the fact that she was going to have to put up with a bunch of smelly soldiers for the rest of her time in Darkonia. Pennie explained what had happened as they strode outside. Along one of the open walkways overlooking the border it would not take long to cross. The problem was more timing, Alveronians were protective of their border and not that she had encountered any yet. Jacob stood higher up on a balcony keeping an eye on them.

Fort Grismor was a large well maintained fortress near the Qakrenarr Pass. It was one of three main gateways between Darkonia and Alveron. The two countries did not see eye to eye, the mountains and rough terrain acted as a natural barrier keeping the peace. Saranon walked up on her own to see Jacob, she was not thrilled about getting close to him after their last encounter, but this had to be done. She stood back, and produced the papers she had rescued from the attack on the Arthrose. Jacob glared down at her, it seemed to be the only facial expression he knew. He took the papers and she turned to leave. Jacob called after her. 'Thank you,' was all he said.

Saranon glanced back then returned to where Pennie was waiting. 'What was all that about?' Her friend asked.

'I found some papers when I was with the Arthrose.'

'You didn't tell me,' Pennie was not impressed.

'It's a form, admitting Princess Antobathia to the camps.'

Pennie looked at her speechless. Since the camps had fallen information had started flooding out about what went on.

Pennie looked serious, 'I wish you had told me earlier.'

Saranon changed the subject, 'I always thought you were suited to the army.'

'Thank you,' Pennie replied in a flat tone.

'So when were you going to tell me?' She asked.

'Do you know how much effort I had to go to, just to get this far?' Pennie raised her voice and Saranon laughed.

Something was gnawing at the edges of her mind it would not let her be and for once it was not the army. It was different to Ollanthia, but it called her just the same. She reached out and it grabbed hold of her even more. She slipped through the walls of the building. It was a smaller Keep than Ollanthia, but it was still a Keep and beckoned to her, wanting her to know. As she passed through the inner layers the army would be alerted, it would have to be quick. She was guessing by the trouble the Keep was going to that she needed to find out. Saranon was kneeling below the stronghold. She waited in the area above the central core where the Keep could communicate to a private audience, if it wished.

She had done this before and wondered if this was why the Keep decided to call on her in this way. It was a warning, a dire one and she knew she would have to act fast. Saranon turned to stand up and almost ended up in Jacob's embrace for the second time. Her look caught him off guard. 'I have to leave now, you are in danger if I stay. It was only meant to be a brief visit,' she looked serene and in control.

For a moment Jacob did not say anything, so she continued, 'Look after Pennie, and if anyone asks I am not Saranon. Your Keep says that if you say otherwise it would not bode well.'

Saranon was about to pass him when he spoke, 'How did you know that the Arthrose Councillors were using dark sorcery?'

'I could see their auras' she went to leave and Jacob hugged her, this time she did not go limp.

She looked up into his eyes and saw that he cared. 'Keep in touch,' was all he said before the Keep showed her out.

Fort Grismor had spoken with a firm tone the Arthrose were travelling fast, she had to make good distance and leave no trace. Saranon made her way back to her belongings and found Pennie sitting at the edge of the bed.

She stopped for a moment, and realised that her friend had packed for her. She hugged her old friend. It was too late for a long goodbye and she knew she had to go soon. She stood with her new robes flowing as she left the room. When Saranon walked by everyone stepped aside and let her pass. She strode out under the starlight in the cool still night. Her heart belonged in Darkonia as she glanced back, hoping this time would not be the last to set eyes upon her homeland.

CHAPTER FIVE

The path to the Summer House

The winds stirred over the damp grass, it was morning and Saranon made her way forward. As she lifted her weight from either foot and strode on. She had managed to pass through the skirmish at the border. She was trying to read the map that Pennie had given her, as the wind flicked at the edges in a playful dance. If the map was right, it would lead her east to a place called the Summer House. The home of Lady Ammera Alvere, a wise sorceress, who helped people on their path. Saranon did not exactly know what her path was, but it sounded like a good first step in this new land. The long winter had taken its toll, she did not have far to go and set up camp for the night in amongst the rocky base of the mountain range.

Pennie had packed plenty of food but she need not have as she was able to look after herself. If she had to buy anything she was good at finding discarded coins and the ground along the border was littered with them. It was not the most glamorous use of sorcery but practical. She used a few sova bags to carry her belongings, including Tellembre, in a small pouch attached to her belt, which also held her talik tucked to the side. She unpacked a sleeping bag and settled in for the night underneath the stars. The fine lines in the earth vibrated and Saranon opened her eyes. It was still dark whatever was coming this way was moving too slow for sorcery.

She stuffed her sleeping bag away and gazed around to see if she could find anything. If someone came across her she had dressed like an experienced traveller. It was uncommon for people to travel in these parts. The large game would rotate throughout the year in an attempt to get away from the local dragons. Saranon moved to take a look, she did not want to be caught off guard, even if it turned out to be nothing. She walked down and straight into the commotion before she realised. They had not noticed yet and she wondered for a moment what would be the best approach. A gruff deep voice said, 'I could have sworn one of them came this way.'

Saranon realised what a fool she had been, they had picked up her use of sorcery. She only knew one approach and that was to dive right in, 'One what?'

She was standing near the middle of the group and they all took a step back as a man made a light sphere so that they could all see. 'Is there any reason for disturbing my sleep?' She continued.

Jameson ignored Saranon's question, 'What are you doing here?'

Saranon produced a passport and permission form granting leave from Darkonia. 'Your outpost was receiving too much attention, so I was going to check in at the Summer House,' she answered.

She thanked Pennie for her smart thinking, her old friend knew she would attract trouble. Riddley looked over Jameson's shoulder astonished. 'You could have come back afterwards, instead of walking through,' he stated.

'That's not my thing,' Saranon tucked her papers away.

The sun was starting to come up and Riddley spoke, 'Well if you're going to the Summer House then you won't mind accompanying us.'

'Much appreciated, I'm terrible at reading maps,' Saranon said before anyone else could get a word in, 'Which is the best way?'

Jameson was not too sure about this, 'First we have to get our belongings.'

She followed the group back to their camp there were twenty in all. She found a couple of mazette dragons to play with and was so wrapped up in the tiny creatures that she just caught the tail end of an argument. The wizards were unsure whether they should travel with her to the Summer House. 'If it's too much trouble I can go by myself,' Saranon said. She walked toward them with one small dragon on her head; one crouched in arm and another on her shoulder taunting the one on her head.

The mazettes were the size of a medium scale birds

and quick to frighten. The sight drew the attention of the soldiers. She wondered what they were all staring at and looked behind her. She could be slow to catch on and was not amused. Jameson decided that they would go with her and she climbed up on an extra horse. Saranon could not think of anything to say, which made the first half of the journey uncomfortable. Every now and then she would catch one of soldiers staring at her and started to wonder what she had gotten herself into.

'So which part of Darkonia are you from?' Jameson said trying to make polite conversation.

'From the north, then I moved around a lot,' she answered. Saranon only had several weeks to get to know Darkonia and she hoped that she was not going to be quizzed.

'What do you plan to do in Alveron?' he asked.

That was a good question she had not thought of and said the first thing that came to mind, 'I was going to meet the Lady Alvere.'

Jameson shook his head in response. She did not know what to say and the rest of the journey hung in a strained silence.

Saranon could see the gates that marked the Summer House up ahead, she had read descriptions of the place from the library at Felgrai. She became nervous, not knowing how the Lady would receive her. It struck her that this was not her homeland as she felt small. Two large stone walls with no actual gate marked the entrance into the grounds of the Summer House. The group rode in on the horses which were beginning to lag, it was a good time for them to rest. She held her emotions in as they led her inside the building. She felt more when she heard Riddley talking with the guard and finding out that she was not expected. The house stood on a small yet powerful Keep, which meant if anything happened she would have an advantage.

An aide came and stated that the Lady Alvere would see Saranon. She did not have a chance to rest and followed the aide into a grand hall. Lady Alvere sat on an elevated platform at the opposite end. The last rays of light filtered through the windows and the light spheres on the walls began to glow as it faded. She walked forward to see Lady Alvere sitting in a clam stance with her eyes closed. The Lady opened them and stared, 'Is this how you plan to take Alveron, too cowardly to show yourself?'

Saranon was stunned, but the Lady continued as she stood close. 'You hide amongst our soldiers, is this how Darkonia takes what it wants?' Lady Alvere demanded.

Saranon was confused, she could not understand. Then it occurred to her that the Lady must think she was connected to the group that had fought at the border, 'I am not with the razen.'

'Of course you are not,' Lady Alvere spat the words out in haste. 'Now that you have the Summer House you will take everything else for your King.'

'No,' Saranon was aghast.

'You cannot fool me!' Lady Alvere shouted.

'I am not. I came here for your guidance.' Saranon's anger showed this was not what she had expected.

She walked away closing the door behind her. She could not go back so instead she found her way down to a small garden, and sat on the bench. What did Lady Alvere mean about taking the Summer House, it did not make sense. Pennie would have known what to do? She looked down at the marks on her hands, and took her jacket off. She stared at the fire mark on her right shoulder, the symbol of the fires of chaos. It had been used by the Arthrose to mark the Issola and a permanent reminder of her childhood. She decided that if Lady Alvere was not going to help, the next task would be to remove the fire mark. She had to find some way of changing the tattoo so it was not an obvious reminder.

Jameson and Riddley felt as though they had just been swept into the middle of a storm. Lady Alvere was so distraught, that Riddley found himself in the unusual position of trying to calm her down. Jameson had gone looking for Saranon and saw the fire mark as she repositioned her jacket. She knew Jameson was there, the Keep told her. She wondered if that was what the Lady had meant 'now that you have the Summer House you will take everything else'. She turned and looked at Jameson who realised that Riddley had sent him on a task far beyond his capability. This had not deterred the experienced soldier before.

He stood in Saranon's way, 'The Arthrose must have trained you well at the camps?'

She felt sick at the memory, 'All I came for was guidance and I was told that you would help.'

'I think you should relinquish the Summer House,' Jameson spoke.

'I haven't got the Keep! I can't relinquish something I don't have!' she exclaimed.

'If the Lady gives you guidance will you go back to Darkonia?'

Saranon stood close, 'I can't I've been exiled.'

Jameson looked into her eyes for a moment. He was a wizard and with one glimpse saw the truth as his stare softened, 'Then you'll need a place to stay.'

'Yes,' she replied.

'Wait here,' with that Jameson left a confused sorceress standing alone in the garden.

Saranon was beginning to wonder if there was a country that would not ridicule her. Jameson came around the corner, 'Lady Alvere will see you now.'

She was about to open her mouth, but thought better of it. She followed the soldier to a drawing room large enough to hold the Lady's personal guards. Lady Alvere continued to glare at her, 'Why would Darkonia exile its most prized possession?'

It took a moment for Saranon to realise that the Lady was referring to her. She thought a moment before she replied, 'Lady Alvere you are the first person I have encountered who does not think I am Issola.'

The Lady laughed, and Saranon did not understand why. 'There have never been Issola.'

'Then may I ask what am I?' Saranon asked.

Lady Alvere took her time she could not convince

herself to believe the girl did not know, 'You are the Angeon.'

Saranon looked puzzled and wondered if Lady Alvere had just made it up. Everyone looked serious, 'I'm sorry, but I don't know what that means.'

Lady Alvere was still unconvinced. 'The Angeon is Darkonia's answer to the Oracle. A sorcerer born with the ability to break down all defences and render a civilisation powerless.'

Saranon thought back to when she broke out of the camp and demolished several others. She had drawn so much energy from the Keep and it had not harmed her. Tasha had known she was unique and took that secret to her grave. She still did not understand. If she was supposed to be a weapon then why was she not like a soldier? It did not make sense.

She went off to bed after a long night. She was exhausted and drifted off to sleep. The Keep hummed away content underneath not minding her presence. The night was filled with strange dreams she kept waking, thinking that people were watching her. She ended up sleeping in the same room as Jameson, the only one brave enough to wake her. They both jumped scaring each other as he shook her shoulder. 'What's wrong with your eyes?' Jameson spoke.

Saranon took a while to focus it felt like she had been in two places at once then came back down to earth. Jameson said, 'It's almost noon.'

'Does Odana mean anything to you?' He did not say anything so Saranon continued, 'It tried to speak to me.'

'You should ask Lady Alvere,' he said with a stern voice.

When she came down to lunch Lady Alvere looked every part the serene figure that Saranon had expected. As they walked in the garden the Lady explained that Odana was an old temple and Keep, located north close to the border with Normisia. Saranon was going to let it be, but Jameson said that it would be a good idea for her to travel to Odana. The nearest place that could offer her proper training was in Serenphel to the far north.

Lady Alvere was polite as she spoke. The Keep sounded talkative so Saranon asked a question and received a reply straight away. No one noticed her brief silence as they walked along. 'Lady Alvere, I am not a threat. This is why the Keep does not react to me.' As Saranon spoke she could tell that was what had been bothering the older sorceress.

Everyone appeared so calm to her and she broke the silence in her clumsy fashion, 'Can you tell me who Odana is?'

Lady Alvere sat down on a stone bench with graceful ease, and she followed. 'Odana is one of the oldest Keeps in the Zyanthian Region and perhaps the largest. Most of his records are gone and we can only estimate his real size. You are not the first Angeon to enquire about Odana he was home for the Angeons of old. Much of our history is lost from the Dreshan Occupation. I cannot tell you what Odana's role in your future will be, nor can I say where it will lead.'

Lady Alvere showed the fear on her face from yesterday.

Saranon found herself thinking that the more she found out the less she realised she knew. It turned out that the people with the most information about the Angeon were the Armythral in Serenphel. A mighty organisation made up by some of the most powerful sorcerers in the region and the world. They preferred not to get entangled in the affairs of other sorcerer clans. Yet the Lady insisted on contacting them. Jameson knew the Summer House well and showed her around. It was reaching the end of winter and in amongst the strange land she began to realise how much she had missed.

At dusk Saranon left the house and crouched under an old tree in the garden. She managed to pick up a signal from the Keep strong enough to dial using her talik. She waited as the thin cool breeze played along her cheeks and fingertips. She almost dropped the device when a signal returned. She placed it on the ground and listened to the familiar sound of Pennie's voice. Telling her what had happened in the short time she was gone. She leaned her head back against the trunk of the tree. Her friend had not heard of the Angeon, but Pennie knew how to find out. Saranon trusted her old friend more than anyone else. Pennie wanted to know what Alveron was like, and started giving advice about a country which she had not seen.

Long after the call had ended, she sat with her eyes closed almost motionless. She could sense Jameson close by and gave no sign of recognition. She walked up to him, startling the man as he said, 'You're a long time out here?' He remarked.

'Has Lady Alvere made contact with the Armythral yet?' She asked.

'Yes, but they do not believe her. The Lady asked me to look for you,' he replied.

She sprinted back to the house, rushing into a circular room where Lady Alvere had opened a doorway to the Armythral. Saranon had seen projected images of people before, but not up close. They looked real and she forgot they could see her as well when she stood close to get a better look. Ryan looked back just as curious; his years of experience told him what he was looking at. Yet there had been no Angeon in Zyanthia since the Dreshan Occupation ended over 200 years ago. The Armythral had almost thought the gene wiped out, or so diluted that it would not produce another. He looked at Saranon, 'You will go to Odana.'

Lady Alvere showed concern, 'Ah you sure that is wise, you are asking something that we do not know the answer to.'

'Odana will be fine, he will know what to do, if she stays here it may attract attention,' he replied.

'I think she already has,' the Lady commented.

'I was referring to something else,' Ryan added.

'You can go now Saranon,' the Lady motioned for her to leave.

With that she left Lady Alvere with Ryan and his colleagues. She was not interested, after talking with Pennie she felt a bit home sick and Ryan would take her further away. She was beginning to wonder if this was such a good idea. She could see Jameson and Riddley with the others preparing to leave the Summer House. It was a beautiful old building rising above the trees in a quiet part of the forest, away from civilisation. It had served her well, but she was itching to move on. The Keep had told her about Alveron. She was quite comfortable letting Lady Alvere feel as though she was in control of the situation. The Lady had been quite clear about Saranon's travel arrangements which suited her. It was the quickest path to Serenphel in the far north.

She only half believed Ryan and Lady Alvere about being the Angeon. She thought of herself as ordinary in the world of sorcery. If it meant an education then she was happy to play along, after all she was not the one who had made the claim. Pennie had not been comforting, and all she had found out was that the bloodline of the Angeon was believed to be dead. This gave her no sign of what the Angeon was meant to be and Saranon did not like not knowing. It had been on her mind and intruded in her sleep. She had heard nothing further from Odana which was just as well. The soldiers were ready to go with their unusual cargo. Jameson took great pride in telling her about the plants and wildlife, as well as Alveron's history.

The landscape was foreign and it was written on her face as they made good pace. She could sense people watching them, a quick glance at Riddley and she could tell he knew who they were. The terrain was a bit drier than what she had seen in Darkonia. A horse was not her normal mode of transport and it felt a little strange. The group pulled off the track to a well-used camp site, as the stars started to arrange themselves in the sky. A fire had already been lit and a man heading towards the group returned Riddley's friendly greeting.

Saranon blended in with the group after having answered enough questions during the day to set the group at ease. Now she sensed a whole new group trying to pick her out. She was sorting out her bed for the night, in one of the tents that had been setup. She could tell two people were standing behind her. She stood up into the harsh stare of man younger and better dressed than Ridley, who was standing close by. Anthony stood tall against the girl, he was higher in authority. She started to wonder if Lady Alvere's words meant anything here. Anthony was from the security forces based at Odana and had been asked to escort Saranon through Alveron. She had the distinct feeling Anthony was not going to be as easy to fool as Max had been. This was not a promising sign for her late night deviations along the lay-lines. He did not look like he was thrilled about the experience either.

After that she stayed close to camp. She hoped that Anthony would keep a comfortable distance. She could feel his eyes staring at her and she was starting to get agitated, but no one seemed to notice. The morning was not much better with Anthony staying close, by now it was obvious Saranon's mood had turned sour. With every step closer to Qwezkin Fort, the nearest Keep, the feeling became stronger. It occurred to her that it was not Anthony that was changing her mood and broke from the party to ride ahead.   He kept a close pace and almost drove his horse over the edge when she stopped on a rise. Saranon had lost all focus in her new chaperon to the point where she had become completely still.

She snapped out of her trance with Anthony shouting and holding her. She was not used to being held by anyone and removed herself from the embrace. She stared at Qwezkin Fort as Jameson asked if she was all right. 'I don't think we should go there,' Saranon explained.

'They know we're coming,' he said.

She was not convinced, but she could not pick up anything unusual about the Keep and carried on. Anthony appeared to lose all memory of helping her, and retained his cold façade. The ground changed into lush fields as they entered a small makeshift town surrounding the Keep. The sun had begun to set, and whatever had changed her mood was gone.

The large group entered into what appeared to be the main checking point inside the building. The foyer was on the south-eastern corner and swung around to Odana Temple in the distance. She wandered off and looked through the tall windows. 'Beautiful isn't it?' The voice came from a lady by the name of Jane.

Anthony and Saranon walked up to the platform where a better view could be seen. Up close Qwezkin seemed much larger, with the ground falling to the east showing below where they had entered.

She leaned over, and watched the dragons getting ready to work in the field below. 'What if I am not this

Angeon?' She asked.

'If you travelled to Serenphel the Armythral would be able to tell,' Anthony spoke.

'That's what I thought,' she mused.

Saranon lost herself in thought and the sky turned into night. She ran down the stairs, holding her left hand out to the wall of the Keep. It took her a moment to realise she was not getting any response. Then Qwezkin was the type of Keep that may not want to say anything. Before she went to bed that night it occurred to her that she should thank Anthony. While looking through her items she found a small protection charm she had made at Ollanthia and offered it in gratitude. He held the small piece in his hand unsure of what to say. He said a curt thank you, with that she drifted off to sleep.

CHAPTER SIX

Saranon woke while it was still dark, she knew she had to act fast. She was careful not to make a sound as she slipped out. According to the Summer House the library was downward and that was where she was heading. It was away from the main areas occupied by the Alveronian Army. Her palms were beginning to sweat as she touched the wall, she was almost there. The side door had several seals on it which faded in her grip and rearranged themselves so that she could enter. The smell was stale as she tiptoed over to an alcove and opened the locked door. She found what she was looking for, just a hand full of books on the Angeon. She did not have time so she held the talik over the books and copied the information which seemed to take for ever. Saranon hoped that the image she had left would be enough to fool Anthony into thinking she was still in bed.

She was heading through the main room when she heard a noise and darted out. In the hallway the air was crisp from a sudden drop in temperature. She touched the wall and felt nothing, all she could sense was silence. Then just as she raised her fingertips a jolt went through her and she was no longer Saranon. She ran following the source of the void, her glowing eyes were enough to keep people from hindering her path. She moved downward through the wall, and straight into danger. Her bond-breaker slashed through three dark sorcerers before the others had time to react. She glided between the sorcerers as they formed around her.

Before she had a chance to strike again, they had begun an attempt to leach her dry of her sorcery. It swelled up and out, ripping them apart and they tried to stop. Qwezkin's thoughts entered her head in a flood. The walls moved as the Keep latched onto her tormentors and sucked their screaming bodies into the Keep. Saranon realised there were people around her screaming and shouting. In the moment she was a fifteen year old girl again and turned to run, thudding straight into Anthony who took her out of the scene. The full impact of what had happened hit her when she saw the wounded, he led her through to a room to be checked.

When she was given the all clear they went back to a small lounge area, where Anthony spoke with his colleagues while she fell asleep. She woke to the smell of scrambled eggs and a hearty breakfast. The Keep sounded less angry, but it was not going to settle down. Saranon sat up and her hands were shaking. He placed her breakfast on a low table then saw the marks on the palms of her hands. 'Where did you get those?'

She realised she had forgotten to cover them up, 'The Arroada gave them to me.'

Harold was a big man who looked like he had just come from working on the Keep. The dirt still stuck to his clothes, as he intruded on the conversation to look at her hands. 'The Armythral won't teach you now. Those marks are given to a sorcerer who has completed more than just the basic training.'

Saranon blurted out, 'But I haven't had any training.'

She realised how naïve she had been. She began to feel sick as it dawned on her that the Arroada had stopped her from training elsewhere.

She stood up and barged her way out. She needed some space and the Keep was not leaving her alone. She heard Anthony in the background. She decided that if she helped the Keep at least she could get time to think, with that she vanished into the wall. Her anger matched the Keep's, as she realised she had come so close, only to have what she wanted taken away. The room fell down into the depths of the Keep far below the ground. Saranon knew Harold spoke true as she sat down resting her head on her knees, crying silent tears that only Qwezkin could hear.

The low hum of the central core started to reveal itself in the background and she stepped out wiping the tears from her face. She had submerged once before and had found the experience quite scary, as she did not like large volumes of water. This time she was filled with anger and the water surrounded her with a cool relief on her burning temper. Then she sank her head beneath and the transformation was complete. Saranon did not believe in mermaids, but if she had to describe her appearance unfortunately this fairy tale would be a close fit. In this form she could build up speed and go to low depths as Qwezkin lit the way. The Keep did not want the Darkonian to get lost any more than she did.

She followed the old lines down and saw the start of the chamber where one of the transit stations lay. She popped her head up above the water and moved at a swift pace. The ceiling, walls and part of the station were caked in gunk. This was where someone's dumped material had ended up. Saranon had seen this sort of thing before and was not afraid to tackle the problem head on with Qwezkin's guidance. She began to wonder if she did need training and the old Alveronian Keep scoffed at such a notion. The work went on for far too long, but at the same time it finished far too fast. She would have to go up and face reality, so she stopped awhile to admire her handy work. It was not the best job in the world, but it would do, and Qwezkin seemed to be satisfied. She asked the Keep a question and it answered while she left the hidden chamber behind.

Saranon had lost four days, she had food, so the time had not worried her. It was night time, and she was about to get ready to curl up into her bed to sleep. Anthony entered, he was smiling, 'There you are, come down and have some dinner.'

He told her that they had been looking for her until Harold realised that she was helping the Keep. 'I needed some time to think,' Saranon said in a calm tone.

He took her answer in his stride. She wondered if it would have made any difference had she said she had been plotting the end of the world. Then she thought better of it, with everything that had happened Anthony may not have taken it so well.

She stopped in the corridor, and the voices in the background seemed to fade away. 'Anthony, I was exiled from Darkonia for executing the Arthrose Council.'

He looked at her, 'I know.'

It was an awkward moment, but it seemed right to say it. Saranon's shoulders slumped down in relief as her body exhaled its secret. She relaxed in the large room with two crackling fires, one at either end warming up the thick stone walls. The scene was filled with the hub of casual conversations. The voices rose in snippets, floating up to her ears, broken by the occasional sound of laughter. She stayed for a while before the tiredness of the last few days flowed down her limbs and went off to a warm cosy bed.

The Keep had gone quiet again, but that was okay. She had the answer she wanted, and she was keen to go off on an adventure. Odana Temple, the beautiful old building lunged up through the walls of the mountain. It marked the corner stone of Darkonia, Normisia and Alveron. The Keep was some distance away, yet his presence was awe inspiring, and it captivated her. Anthony for all his experience, had not had to babysit an Angeon before and she was about to take full advantage of this. The open plain was too obvious so she headed down. There were a few old tunnels linking Qwezkin to Odana which were dangerous for the ordinary person.

Saranon saw this as an open invitation, after all, she had grown up in camps and all that hardship had to be of some use. She covered the great distance with ease, the tunnels were much quicker. She clambered up into one of the main chambers, its ancient columns reaching high above in a circular fashion. Her eyes continued straight up above and she felt her talik buzzing. With a sigh she picked it up and wondered if her life was ever meant to be peaceful. She looked down at her talik; it was downloading a massive amount of data at a fast rate. She could see the living energy of Odana in her peripheral vision it was much stronger than anything she had come across.

The groaning and creaking of the old Keep gave a strange, eerie sensation that tingled down her spine and made her hands quiver. She looked around still holding the talik in her hand, glancing at the shadows that moved in an unnatural fashion. The floor had been carved in some long forgotten pattern which made its way up to the tall ceiling. There were signs of grand images that had once detailed the walls, the only hint of colour stuck deep in the odd crevice. Saranon thought it was odd to find no dust, the air was fresh and apart from its age, the chamber was clean. She held her hand up against the wall. It felt warm with a distant dull hum which flowed through her fingers holding her in a trance. She felt someone touch her shoulders and she jumped, when she turned there was no one there.

She began to wonder if she had made a mistake coming here and turned to leave. She tried to open the door, but it would not budge. Saranon stood back trying to figure out what was going on and hid near a corner behind one of the columns, peering out. She could not sense anything and wondered what was happening. She tried communicating with the Keep, but nothing came back. In an instant the lights came on and it was not the Keep. Saranon knew that was not a good sign. She could feel her heart start to pound in her chest and her palms sweat. She was in another country, but this felt too familiar.

The air began to warm up and she knew she was in trouble as the sensation prickled up her arms. The sound of steps came closer toward her, conflicting with the sound of her heart beat as it beat hard in her chest. The shadows moved around her as they began to blur her vision, and she was pushed into the centre of the chamber by an unseen force. The patterns on the floor moved and she thought she had to be imagining it. She stood up and could almost make out twelve figures around her. She could not make out what they were saying.

Somehow her hearing along with her vision had become distorted and a single thought came to her mind. What if this is what happened to Tasha? She plunged herself down, ripping apart the stone floor with a force beyond all comparison. Her energy tore hard into keep breaking and melting the floor away with the steady impact. The Keep relented in agony and she fell into the darkness below. She could hear the boom of the floor breaking behind her and then she saw a strange glow that headed towards her like a sprawling web. Then something grabbed her and pulled her down so fast that everything became a blur.

She fell into a peaceful trance, somehow whatever had hold of her, felt comforting and much safer than the people in the chamber. Saranon kept on heading downward and wondered if it would ever stop. Tiny shards of reality started filtering through, whatever was above her had started catching up. She looked up to an awesome sight, made up of something that resembled an elaborate glowing spider web. The furtherest tendrils of the web shot out toward her. Its tiniest points fast trying to grasp the girl, her body jarred with the sensation of pain poised on the tips of the web. Her energy rang out with one final blast, disintegrating the edges as the web recoiled. It broke and shattered as it hit the edges of the tunnel.

The air grew warm and something deep beneath her rose up around, she could see the end of the tendrils begin to curl away. A giant dull hum spread out around her and the falling sensation along with the pain had gone. In all the turmoil she had closed her eyes. She held out her hands and felt around to get up, she realised there was nothing beneath her. In a state of shock she opened her eyes and found herself floating near the top of a massive underground chamber. Its spherical walls loomed down in the darkness extending off into nowhere. For some unknown reason the ancient walls had not heard about a little thing called gravity. The sparks of light crackled every now and then, from the grey clouds swirling in the depths below.

Odana had lived for 1227 years and for a small moment the Angeon saw him or thought she did. In the glimmer of the depths below in the midst of the whirlpool raging like a thunderous storm, its mass had revealed itself above. While keeping the swirling matter trapped beneath its grasp and then as just as it appeared, it had gone. Saranon's mind was overloading with the impossibility of what she saw, it had to be a dream that was the only way she could explain it. The age old core hurled an invisible force upward and hurled her back to the world of humans.

In the darkness that followed all Saranon could sense was the energy of the Keep, as it lifted her up with a might she could not comprehend. She held her eyes closed, not wanting to see where she was, but she knew she had to. She glimpsed the last remnant of Odana's work as he melded the floor back in place. The chamber appeared empty, as though nothing had happened. She stumbled as she tried to move, falling back onto the floor as she rolled over and stared up at the ceiling. It reached on forever in the darkness of the great chamber, as she peered up the shadows moved as though taunting her from a distance.

She was too exhausted to move as every muscle in her body ached and her head spun. The creaking sounds of the great Keep filled the emptiness, not letting her rest. Something brushed against her skin, but when she turned her head, nothing was there. An echo rang out from the distance, carrying voices with it as the sounds edged closer.

Saranon could sense the wizards approaching, but she was too exhausted to shout, as no sound came out. She never thought she would be so glad to see them, and managed a smile before falling into a deep slumber.

She was held in a troubled sleep. It stretched just underneath the surface of her consciousness. Her mind overloading with images of the great darkness and what lay beneath. Every time she tried to focus the image kept returning to the sensation of falling. She held out her hand to grab hold and this time she clutched something real. All at once her senses reacted and brought her back to reality. Saranon found herself gripping Anthony's jacket in clenched fists. As she realised what she had done he embraced her tight to his chest, not wanting to let go. She had the sudden thought that hugging a wizard was not the safest thing to do and ended the union. Anthony did not seem fazed.

It seemed like everyone had known what had happened except her. For the first time she saw members of the Mercidian Council, the Alveronian counterpart for the Arthrose. Lady Alvere had been the first sorceress she had come across in this strange harsh environment along the other side of the border. Saranon ached from her ordeal, as she stumbled around she realised there was something missing. She looked down at her hands and the marks were gone. Their meaning still remained a mystery. They had made her feel uncomfortable and for some strange reason she knew that they were wrong.

'Hello there,' a friendly warm voice spoke belonging

to Clara who was not much older than herself. 'I hear we missed the excitement.'

Saranon looked around to see a mass of bright red hair attached to Clara, the daughter of Flynn. Flynn was a gruff old man with a friendly smile, which Clara had inherited. Clara was more than happy to explain what had happened, as the two made their way around the commotion. They sat down on one of the large window openings, wide enough to sit on, and look out into the beautiful landscape. She was still feeling a bit queasy, and the story from Clara was not making her feel any better.

'The sorcerer clan believe they deserve a claim on several Keeps because they descend from the Otturin. They have been trying to reignite something which already exists within the Keep.'

Clara stopped to pause, 'Do you remember anything?'

'I remember being in the chamber. Then pounding, like huge continuous blows. I was trying to get away and then I fell.' Saranon shrugged her shoulders and sighed looking out the window.

Even though there was plenty of work going on around them, there was not much they could do. She did not feel like running off, she was completely exhausted and it was not fun anymore. She had gone along treating everything like one big adventure, which had been fine until this had happened. She looked around and even Anthony was oblivious to her presence which was far from the truth. The great old Keep creaked and groaned like an old fortress made by many hands rather than by sorcery, one of the signs giving away its age. In the end all things had to die. It seemed like a horrible thought, thinking back about Tasha. Clara was happy to do all the talking, which was fine, as her head still ached from the fall.

Her ears pricked up when Clara referred to the Regent, 'A what?' Saranon asked.

'A Regent, silly me I forgot. You don't have one of those in your country,' Clara was being cheeky.

This started a new conversation, as the day aged she could feel a cold change sweep across Odana. With the cooling of the air she shrugged it off. Clara had since gone with Flynn and she was left to her own devices, she had not gone far trying to blend into the busy background. Saranon was watching the tenants of the Keep, which included the army operating the big old Keep from small screens. The room looked somewhat like a platform of vibrant activity, with people worrying about things she did not understand.

A light from the corner of her eye caught her attention and she peered down. She had chosen a seat in the corner near a bench, but now it had a small light on it. She was filled with curiosity, 'Anthony, what's that?'

He came over, leaning over her shoulder. Without looking she sensed something was wrong. 'I'll let Riddley know,' he started walking away and added, 'Don't touch the...'

Saranon had her finger on the little light, and the whole bench flickered into life with strange symbols. Then she saw it.

She could understand, right in the middle, she placed

her hands near it leaning over. Strange three-dimensional patterns in long continuous streams flittered by before her eyes. The sensation stirred something inside. The word fell out of her mouth, 'Intruders.'

Riddley had managed to pinpoint the breach, he was not impressed. Anthony led her away from the unfolding drama and told her to get some rest. She thought that was rather a contradiction, but went anyway.

After the minor events of that night things went back to a mundane routine in the Keep. Saranon spent time with Clara and a wizard by the name of Derek whom she suspected was filling in for Anthony. Either way, the west was full of old ruins from where the three countries met and had been an empire with its heart in the east. The majestic stones that were fading underneath her feet, made her wonder what the Angeon would have been like back then. The information from the Summer House and Qwezkin had been useful, but it was still a small drop in a deep lake.

She asked, 'If this place was the centre of Zyanthia then would any great vault of knowledge be left?'

'I'm afraid not, the history we have left makes reference to your ancestors, but little more. Any information recorded by the Otturin would have passed to the Shalough, and they do not share.'

'They have chosen to restrict access. You could ask Lady Alvere.' Derek said.

Saranon was not so warm to the idea as the Lady had not exactly been forthcoming. There had been a lack of high level sorcerers in west Alveron and that had been a relief.

It had taken her longer to recover than she thought and she still felt weak, almost as if she were going backwards. The day had been long and her bones ached from a journey that should not have given her any worry. During the night her dreams haunted her, as they had since the incident. She could see herself falling, being dragged below. Then she was floating she opened her eyes only this time was different. By the thinnest thread she used all her strength to break through. At first she could hear herself screaming, then her consciousness caught up and she was gasping for breath. She remembered and her body reeled in shock. She tried to move and someone was holding her tight it took her a moment to realise. Saranon stopped screaming, but could not cope, 'I can't…' she gulped, 'I can't handle it.'

Anthony managed to hold her down until she sobbed, the commotion had woken Clara and Flynn's voice, told her to stay away. Flynn waited until she had calmed a little. 'If you do that again there will be serious consequences.' Flynn said.

'I saw the central core,' Saranon whispered.

The room fell silent. Flynn leaned down and in a gesture of kindness kissed her on the head. Her body was exhausted and out of need more than anything, she slipped back into sleep.

Her memories had rearranged themselves in the right place, Clara stayed close by her side. Saranon had spent most of yesterday down in the medical centre, only to find out the best thing was to do nothing. She was just going to have deal with it on her own. After growing up in the camps that was not a huge problem. She had the impression that if she had been anyone else, they would have bent over backwards to help. In a way she could understand fearing the unknown. The amount of energy she had let off in the Keep had been hidden by the central core from the outside world.

Anyone inside the Keep who could sense sorcery had noticed. Saranon laughed as she still saw strange looks as she strode by, she was not going to be able to hide in the corner anymore. Flynn had apologised, but in the same sentence he managed to make it clear that doing that sort of thing in the west was not appropriate. Odana lay close to two borders, Darkonia to the west and Normisia to the north. When she closed her eyes all she saw was the image. She had tried telling Clara, but the words would not come out. So she stayed in limbo waiting for the shock of it all to pass.

CHAPTER SEVEN

Odana Temple

The winds swept around the mountainside making hollow remarks. It rumbled down the massive air vents and into the body of the Keep. The structure was a fine-tuned mechanism with an almost seamless operation. A repair crew was sent down to fix the latest damage from intruders, who had managed to wreck some of the cabling, leading to the lower systems on the eastern side. The outer doors to the area were still working and had been locked. The Keep lay close to the border and this made it difficult to deal with breaches. Too much energy would draw the wrong sort of attention.

Still the occupants had become quite innovative; Saranon could not help but be impressed. The bulk of the Keep was well hidden in the mountain range and went unnoticed. There was a sense of urgency about getting the repairs done and she could see that they were not going well. Derek being younger had been put to the task of carrying tools backwards and forwards. The repair crew was so busy that at times they had almost asked her by mistake. For some reason asking, her was not considered appropriate and she did not question why. By the end of a hot day in the confines of the Keep, a couple of the crew showed their frustration. Their efforts had not gone as well as they had hoped.

The whole sense of formality had gone a few hours ago and it was starting to get late. Clara was talking to Shaun who was leading the repairs. This time he was a little calmer. Clara came over and said 'The area near ground level on the eastern side is down, which means we won't know if there is another attack. How do you feel about a long night?'

Saranon did not answer for a while, she felt like she was missing something and she was not the only one who could sense it. She knew what Clara meant, ever since she remembered the central core. There had been questions on how much access she had to the Keep.

In the sorcerer community it was like striking gold, but she did not see it that way. If she did have a higher level of access, then she was obligated to be careful how she used it. She felt like she was being coerced, but a breach of this scale was serious. The Keep would want it fixed, 'I'll have a look that's all.'

Clara restrained her excitement and Saranon wondered what she had gotten herself into.

The time had become late and with part of the Keep down, except for basic functions, the building took on an eerie feeling. In the silence the wind could be heard gusting down the large vents placing everyone on edge. There was a small tapping noise, Shaun cautioned Derek who replied under his breath, 'That wasn't me.'

She could see Shaun motion with his hands giving out orders, she had two choices stay in this world or step back into the other.

She called Clara close and unwrapped the jet black bond-breaker Odayour, the twin of the one she had given Pennie. It remained stable in the form of a small dagger. She passed it to Clara who for a moment did not understand, 'I made it, take it and go back, it's yours.'

'This is too much I can't,' Clara held it with such care. Anyone would have thought Saranon had given her much more than just a small homemade artefact.

Clara tried to hand it back, and Saranon reached out to stop her, 'I made it, I get to choose. It stays with you, now go.'

Derek stayed behind, he was too young for this, but then so was she. She tried to turn, but something was holding her back and she grunted in shear frustration. Then a thought entered her head and she leaned over near Derek, 'I want you to hit me.'

'What?' Derek looked puzzled.

She rolled her eyes before explaining, 'I meant wizardry, not your fist.'

He understood, but was not looking too keen on

the idea. He did not seem in a hurry to oblige so Saranon started walking toward Shaun. A searing pain thumped the breath out of her chest, she wanted to laugh and cry at the same time. She crumpled to the ground clenching her muscles and holding back a scream that pounded inside her head.

By now the area was filling with people who were positioning themselves to guard the area for the night. In the middle of this she transformed into her true self. Hundreds of voices flittered through her head which had been recorded in the walls of the Keep. She tried to contain the pressure. It was almost an invisible struggle in the darkness, but Saranon knew she had to let someone else in. Between clenched jaws she managed to call Shaun over, who was still trying to work by the small illuminated lights. She could not explain and hoped that the experienced wizard would understand. She translated the images and transferred them across through his skin in a painless process. The weight of it all was beginning to show.

Shaun held her and from somewhere she could hear him say 'let go'. The pressure turned off like a tap and she lay for a moment on the ground. Shaun checked her eyes, 'Be careful who you show that to.'

Then he engulfed himself in his work and the rest of his crew worked hard to get the area back on line. The work was going well. She sat near Derek who had apologised for getting a little too enthusiastic with the amount of force he had used. He became more relaxed and the two spoke as the others worked on around them. The power was restored with the growing flicker down the hall as the light came on. The pleasant sound of the equipment firing up filled everyone with a sense of relief.

Saranon went over to congratulate Shaun, when she noticed a small light on the control panel over his shoulder. She had seen it before and her puzzled expression caused Shaun to turn. 'Oh!' He signalled to the others.

For a moment she was expecting him to shout in frustration. Instead everyone around her flew into motion. Derek called her over and she stayed down close by. She could make out Anthony up ahead and she wondered why Flynn was not present. That thought faded as it dawned on her what the strange looking light had meant.

By now it was obvious Derek had been left behind to baby-sit as she let out a frustrated sigh. Saranon's senses were still prickling from the energy that had glowed so bright inside her. She turned to face him, 'Sorry Derek.'

Time was running thin as she melted into the background before Derek's eyes. The smell came to her first, the horrible stench of failure wafting up to her nose, crisp and sharp. A soldier lay wounded near her on the floor, but he knew not to make a sound.

She was further down at ground level the most vulnerable area. There were a few shouts from around the corner, but wizards preferred not to make noise so the shouting meant it was getting ugly. The intense energy raging nearby acted like an invisible door that had slammed shut. As she approached, the images which had crammed her head trickled into place. The small drops of reality washed away her fear. Saranon stepped through the haze as she noticed Clara, and tapped her on the shoulder. The two exchanged silent words and Clara followed her forward.

She could not help thinking that they were much alike. She knew the next motion had to be fluid and the adrenalin rushed through her relaxed poise as she ran out into the open area. Charging through the mass of soldiers, she could see Anthony ahead as he fell. She launched herself up behind him stomping his body to the ground. Tellembre in all its glory flexed into the great sword that she had made in chambers below Ollanthia. The blade sliced like a steaming knife into Anthony's attacker turning the sorcerer to dust. She landed on top of the ashes, her nostrils flared with excitement.

Saranon could sense the other attackers getting away. She stormed after them leaving Anthony and Clara behind. The two remaining attackers went down before they had made it outside. The thrill rushed through her veins and she realised it was the Keep's emotions she was sensing. She went back to find Clara looking at the markings on a sorcerer they had managed to capture. By the look on the soldiers who held their captive down, Saranon knew the sorcerer was going to pay a high price for his deeds. The mess was cleared up. As she learned that the Mercidian had been told not to intervene because it had been considered an 'ordinary' matter.

Flynn came down to meet them and hugged both girls the man was like a gentle giant, 'Enough excitement for you two!'

Sorcerers attacking were Mercidian territory. Flynn got straight into assessing the whole situation. Flynn had a lot of questions for her, but at no stage did he raise his voice or chastise her for what she had done. Eight soldiers had lost their lives in a small community that hit many hard and that knowledge lay behind Flynn's silent gaze. Saranon clambered up into the main area and could still feel the thrill of the Keep as she closed her eyes and went to sleep.

Eight dead was not normal for an internal conflict and it reflected the Mercidian's mistake. Flynn was trying to make the best out of a bad situation while doing his job. The girls had been allowed to talk about their ordeal and this helped ease some of the tension within the Keep. Saranon went to see Anthony who was recovering to find him chatting away with several friends. She sat lost for words, and Anthony placed his arm around her. It was hard to see him like that, knowing that she had stomped on him as well did not help.

In the silence of the wizard's embrace she heard him, Odana in the background whispering to her. Anthony's facial expression changed it was as though he heard the whispering too, they're coming. It was a soft spoken voice, but Saranon knew what it meant. She was too close to Darkonia and with the recent events it would be easy to know where she was. She did not want to leave, but deep down she knew she had stayed too long. Anthony saw the look in her eyes, 'You have to go, don't you?'

'Yes,' she replied.

He reached into a little draw beside him. He produced

a small wallet containing an Alveronian passport, 'You might need this.'

She was speechless and she thought to herself perhaps she should tread on wizards more often. The gift was much appreciated and she admired it for ages turning it backwards and forwards. It was held in a small suede wallet, died purple for the colour of Alveron, with a tiny silver clasp which closed together. Shaun who had been sitting close by spoke, 'When things calm down we hope to see you back this way.'

'Definitely,' Saranon responded with gratitude.

The afternoon sun shone in through the small windows high up in the long room as Saranon made an effort to enter in silence. A few coughs broke the air as she stood to the rear of the gathering, as the wizards said their final goodbyes to their fallen comrades. The funeral went on as she sighed underneath her breath with a heavy tone. The atmosphere weighed on her as the funeral gave a fitting end to those who had been lost. It brought home to her the reality of her own struggle.

Flynn explained to Saranon that Clara was so excited over having her own bond-breaker. She had given her new friend a massive status symbol. Now was perhaps not the time to tell Flynn that she had made another while at Odana Temple. She headed back to her room and Clara helped her pack with an enthusiasm that amazed her. Her friend advised her with great confidence on what to expect while travelling north. The Pendelon Plains were arid except along the Cravese mountain range. It was best to follow this to the north then go up through Magladen to Balquene.

The first part of her journey was filled with small farming towns. These were inhabited by wiccan and ordinary folk alike. The wiccan community were reasonable people and as long as she did not try to hide or cause trouble, they would be no trouble to her. Saranon had little to do with wiccan and was not as confident as her new friend.

Flynn became nervous even though the border was a short distance away. Saranon felt restless and so did the Keep, she did not understand what all the fuss was about. It seemed so simple, there was the border she would cross it and be on her merry way. Outside the sky was grey and murky the wind rippled through her cloak, as the weather reflected her inner frustration. A dark sullen mood caressed her fingertips as she held onto the outer wall, moving further down to her heart. The wind swept up over the lookout near the top of the Keep, blasting ice cold air across her face.

Saranon could feel the central core whirring deep below, Odana felt it and so did she. In a calm stance she turned to Flynn who had been gazing out, and spoke, 'You were right.'

Flynn gave her a confused glance, then a big roar shot overhead. In the brief moment that the massive body of the marmoz dragon loomed above, she ran over and pushed Flynn to the ground. It came so close she thought she could see the underneath of its belly. In the dense noise that cluttered the air she said, 'I have to go!'

Flynn nodded.

The next great dragon swung close and this time she clung on yanking herself up, while throwing both dragon and rider off edge. The beast tried to shake her by slamming his hulk against the side of the Keep. Saranon could hear the screams of the rider as he fell, though it was not far. She clung on with her ice cold fingers grasping the soft skin of his belly. The dragon thrust again, this time scraping his leg. In the realisation that the beast had hurt himself, she heaved herself into the saddle. The memories from the old Keep signalled for the dragon to leave. Its great muscular body jumped with immense grace into the air so fast, it took her a moment to realise where she was going.

His path conflicted with the other riders. This caused mounting confusion among the dragons around her. Saranon hoped this would be enough to help Flynn, because she was too scared to stop now. As if sensing her desperation the dragon continued flying into the night. Katholomu flew until he had made his way well across the border, to the south-east of Normisia. He landed in the outskirts of the large city of Dreverdon. The magnificent black dragon drank his fill then curled up in a shallow cave.

Dreverdon was a hub of civilisation where she found she could blend into the background. The busy streets passed her by as she crossed to the other side. Following the lay-lines north she managed to completely bypass several of the smaller towns. She headed into the second largest city Redadere. Her supplies from the markets at Dreverdon had faired her well. Now she had to restock and a nice warm bed was starting to sound good. Saranon found herself walking up to one of the many average looking taverns, and buying a room for the week. The food downstairs though nothing special tasted much better than her cooking and gave her a chance to relax.

Redadere was full of unusual visitors, so she fell right into place. The hard travelling had worn her out and she thought her stay would end up being longer. As she felt the throb of her weary feet underneath the table, she knew that sorcery was not going to fix it. The small bed upstairs was soft and cosy compared to the ground outside and she soon fell into a heavy sleep. Mrs Harper, a nice lady that had seen better years and had not lost her smile, ran the place with her older children helping out. The outer city was made up of swept cobble streets and close-knit buildings. Not the cleanest Saranon had seen, but the people took pride in where they lived.

The seaport brought in a decent turnover that flowed down through the city. The work was not easy, but it kept the city going and made it a vibrant place. As she looked around, it amazed her how a whole mass of people could embrace something so mysterious and unfathomable. The dark swirling green colour peering back from below the dock where she stood, did not appeal to her at all. The map showed no oceans between Redadere and Serenphel. So she could keep her feet planted on dry ground.

The main mode of transport on land was by cart. Not exactly as agile as the misquew and for her using the lay-lines travelling to large distances, was not a problem. The misquew were stubborn and proud. Clara the ever quick thinker had managed a novel way of delivering a message without addressing it to Saranon. It had arrived by mail and by the look on Mrs Harper's face, she was used to strange parcels turning up. The parcel had been addressed to her room number via Mrs Harper. She had spoken to Clara the first day and had taken great care to avoid the call being traced.

Clara wrote that Odana Temple had settled back down, but she should not come back anytime soon. The Shalough sorcerer clan had reacted in a strange manner towards Saranon's presence in Alveron. No one knew why and that was not a good sign. Clara had included a few contact details of people to call. Saranon's last experience while following her friend's advice, had not met with a warm reception. She had been a good friend, and perhaps she would be lucky the second time. She had tried contacting Pennie. Her friend was either too far away, or could not get a direct line back to Darkonia, which meant trying to make contact from a Keep.

The place was littered with small ones and the larger Keeps were well guarded. Walking up and dialling in the talik was not as easy as it sounded. For all its openness the city was well fortified and the port itself had its own complex set of rules. Mrs Harper's daughter Celia was more than happy to get out of her chores by showing Saranon around the city. She felt like she was being let into a strange and enchanting new world, as Celia introduced her around. It was not until she met one of Celia's older friends, a young man by the name of Jedd, the realization dawned on her that they were wiccan.

It was then that she remembered Clara's advice, since she was on her own she had to take care to treat the community with respect. A lone sorceress did not have the luxury of hiding behind a large group. Since she was some sort of anomaly, if she got herself in serious strife she could not count on anyone to come to her rescue. In Jedd's presence she hesitated then let the moment go by. If Saranon was alone in this new world then she would make her own rules and besides she saw no need to be high and mighty. She did not come from an influential background and did not remember much of her past, so there was no need to pretend to be something else.

Though the question had not been asked, she made little attempt to hide herself in amongst the wide variety of people in the city. She had not stood out as being unusual. Soon she realised why Mrs Harper had been so happy to let her go with Celia and smiled. She had been led astray, but not without her consent. Celia and Jedd introduced her to their community. What started out as the odd one or two soon turned into much more. Most of the people were from humble backgrounds. Though she had been isolated from the world at large, hardship was an understood language.

Saranon felt thankful for the fact that she had not been raised among the sorcerers, spread throughout Darkonia. She could not help but sense the irony, and wondered if the Arthrose had ever meant this to be. Celia and Jedd moved around her little room, glancing around at her belongings.

The sova bags included more than she had owned before in her life.

Jedd saw Tellembre fastened in its sheath in the dormant form of a dagger. He held it as he asked, 'This is an elegant piece of craftsmanship, where did you get it?'

Saranon could feel her cheeks growing red, 'I made it.'

Jedd looked at what he held with even more curiosity, 'This type requires skill are you sure?'

'I had some help,' she replied.

Jedd was astounded and she continued, 'I have been told that only a few can make bond-breakers.'

Celia liked the personal treasures that she had found while travelling from Dreverdon. She had grown a habit of collecting lost belongings hidden to other passers-by. Most of the objects were jewellery and small trinkets. Nothing she needed, but the camps had starved her of such fine things and now she found them cluttering up what space she had. Celia fell in love with a few small pieces and without much pleading made them her own. Jedd found Saranon's talik and to her surprise opened the seal unlocking it quicker than she could. He asked, 'This is state of the art how did you get this?'

'My friend Pennie gave it to me so we could keep in touch.'

Jedd played with it in his hands keeping it just out of Saranon's reach. Of course if she wanted to there were other ways of getting it back. Clara had warned her about using sorcery in Normisia.

'You have a lot of information stored in here,' Jedd

looked up at her.

'Yes, but I haven't been able to access most of it.'

Jedd looked as though she had just invited him to a challenge he was happy to accept, 'Leave it with me.'

Before Saranon could say anything the wiccan had pocketed one of her most prized possessions. Although she felt lost without it, Saranon hoped that Jedd would be able to decipher the information, the great old Keep had left behind in the talik. Her own attempts had led her around in circles and she was not one for being patient.

CHAPTER EIGHT

Mrs Harper's Tavern

The night air was warm and thin, with the smell of the ocean wafting in through the window. Tasha's death had left Saranon with a mix of disturbing dreams, which unsettled her senses as she tried to sleep. Her hands opened and closed holding nothing. Somehow the image had stayed with her much longer than any other and filtered through her mind and body. In her dreams she was resting on a stone slab and Tasha was leaning over holding her hand. She looked up into the shell of an old temple with a stream and garden visible from the openings to the side. Tasha had long fawn coloured hair resting on her shoulders, which slipped forward as she spoke; you have to go now you are needed.

She opened her eyes, she was already dressed. The stars outside shone bright as she made her way down the balcony and onto the ground. Her senses spoke to her in a language only she could understand. The weather was warmer this far north of the border, the sea breeze was a welcome gift blowing along her arms. Her senses were more alert than they had been for weeks. Odana had taken its toll, but now she was back to her old self. Saranon felt as though she could waste no time. She dashed across the shadow filled streets dodging the occasional passer-by. Her target was further away on the outskirts, as her silhouette raced through the air without leaving a trace.

Her pace quickened as the energy inside her came to life and ran burning through her system. In that instant she transformed and this time she was in control. Her senses had led her to an older building worn with age, as the first signs of what she was after came floating up to her ears. It pierced through an internal roar from the build up inside. Beautiful and serene the Angeon moved through the wall and down into the chaos below. The screams and sobs from the victims melted into the background noise as Saranon focused on the real reason why she was here. She could feel Tellembre stir underneath her hand, but this time she needed to leave no trace of any bond-breaker. This time it would be for real.

The last few occasions had been haphazard much to her disgust. She had used the time at Odana to concentrate her efforts on accepting what she had become. It had not been easy, then again it never was. The musty smell of sweat stained the air and made her feel queasy inside. This was only a minor distraction as she set sight on her first target.

The thrill made her too excited and again she lost control. Her hold slipped and with that she finished the task with too much haste. She had taken down the main offenders almost in one blow. Her only solace was that this would add more confusion to what had happened to them. She knelt gathering her thoughts in the night air, the victims were free with some injured. Though she could not go back and help them, it was too dangerous.

She cringed at her mistake, it had been an improvement, but still she had failed. It was taking longer than she expected, perhaps she would have to pay more attention to the information from the Summer House. She wanted to have some grasp over her true self before she arrived in Serenphel, so at least she would not be an easy target. The sweat grew cold as it travelled down her spine, and Saranon knew she had to get back. The warm air caked her clothes with sweat and soaked her hair. She thought that the task would be easy, but it turned out to be difficult. She felt her true self taunting her from the shadows, this was not her first encounter, nor would it be her last. Her limbs ached and by the time she made it back, the small bed could not have felt any better.

The first light beaded through the tiny holes frayed in a random pattern over the old curtain. She woke feeling refreshed, with no signs of what had happened during the night. The smells of a most hearty and welcome breakfast wafted up from down-stairs. With that, the previous events were all but forgotten. Saranon was in a deep ponderous thought when the outer world broke her concentration,

Celia came bursting in. By now she had become used to the fact that her room was considered a public space. Celia marvelled in surprise when Saranon was always expecting her spontaneous arrival.

The odd pair had become friends. Celia who had not travelled much was mesmerised by every mundane little detail of Saranon's journey. 'Am I looking at this wrong?' She exclaimed in frustration at the book.

'Of course you are. Sorcerers think of themselves as being different.'

'Then how am I supposed to figure this out, and don't tell me I need to ask a sorcerer.'

Celia held back a laugh, 'I think you need to act like one.'

Saranon looked up from the book, and frowned.

'Yes a bit like that, you find wiccan frustrating.'

'No, but you do party late into the night. I thought that was supposed to be for sleep.'

Celia held her head back in laughter, 'I had about as much sleep as you did!' and gave her a knowing stare.

She hesitated, 'Okay so I'm having a few difficulties.'

'I'm not picking on you. It's just that you saved Jedd's cousin,' Celia replied.

Saranon did not know whether to laugh or cry. 'I hope I'm not being noticed in the sorcerer world.'

'I doubt it, they're only interested when you do something wrong. The problem is they can turn a blind eye far too much,' Celia responded.

Saranon chose to change the subject, 'So how do I act

like a sorcerer?'

This seemed to open up a wide door, as Celia took full advantage of leading her to this particular question. She soon found herself off down the road to where Jedd's Uncle and Aunt lived.

The most esteemed Lord and Lady Karager were proud the owners of Bellington Castle. The grand building was perched on the rise of a small hill overlooking the city. The aged building had a simple splendour which made it stand out from a distance well before they arrived. The place for all its finery was quite welcoming, perhaps because it doubled as a learning centre and was full of life. The long corridors wrapped around the internal courtyard. This opened up to the cool breeze which skimmed along the surface of the pond and kept the atmosphere pleasant. Although the small community pretended not to notice, her presence was felt. She could already feel herself sticking out.

She had not seen so much in Alveron because she had been amongst her own. Now she was aware that she had been blessed in a strange way. It seemed that no matter where she went, as if by luck her path was never blocked, no matter how crowded the place was. This tiny little detail began to annoy her as it prevented her from blending into the background. She was trying hard to be respectful, but it was becoming difficult. Jedd who had joined them could see the frustration on Saranon's face and told her not to worry. They walked up to a small study nestled away to the side of the large lounge area.

Jedd was quite at home here, Celia had explained that Lady Karager was Jedd's mother's sister. Although Jedd's family were not well off that did not bother Lord Karager who welcomed them to work on the estate. Lady Karager and Emily, Jedd's mother were almost inseparable. So no one batted an eyelid when Jedd acted as though he owned the place. The small study was neat with fine yet simple furnishings from the window, she could still see the courtyard below. Jedd was in his element, 'What do you think?'

'Are there that many people here?'

Jedd came over to the window and smiled, 'That's only a small number.'

'I wonder if Indarin in Serenphel will be like this,' she pondered.

'I doubt it your kin make a habit of doing things in a different way. It's a wonder none of them have visited you.'

'I think I know why,' Saranon spoke with a hint of sadness.

Jedd looked at her, 'Being isolated from your own kin is not a good thing.'

Saranon knew what Jedd was referring to and knew that it did not make a difference. The Mercidian, as in Flynn, had left her with an important detail that her centre of learning was internally driven. This meant that it would be easy for her to learn at least nature had blessed her there. 'I'm sure I'll be fine,' she spoke.

Celia who had been quiet for a while, re-joined the conversation, 'He's serious Saranon.'

'So am I,' she spoke a little harsher than she meant to.

Celia gave Jedd a worried look, then Jedd spoke, 'If that is true, which I doubt, then your kin have made a mistake.'

With that the topic turned to Jedd's cousin Reida, who was still recovering from her ordeal that Saranon had rescued her from. The young girl had been injured and her parents had kept most people from seeing her. She wondered what would have happened if she had not been there, then left that thought behind. She could not become weighed down by sentimental things if she was going to be of any use. The most important thing was to figure out how to control her sorcery.

From what she heard Reida had been targeted and Saranon began to wonder if she wanted to know the sorcerers in Normisia at all. Even in her own country the attack had been sorcerer against sorcerer, not sorcerer against wiccan. Somewhere deep down she knew it was not right. It weighed on her mind as she wandered down the long corridors, careful not to bother anyone as she went. For a learning centre for wiccan, the place had an awful lot of information about sorcery, a whole section was devoted to it in the library. She led her fingers along the titles and realised she was looking at the Normisian part. She moved along kneeling down to find the Darkonian section, and found a group she had not heard of before, the Tarquerin.

She sat on the floor turning the pages, and Jedd slouched down, 'You can sit at the table if you like.'

'Oh sorry,' Saranon rummaged through the snippets

of information. 'I haven't come across the Tarquerin.'

'That's not surprising they keep to themselves,' he replied.

She looked up first at Celia then at Jedd 'Celia said you might be able to help.'

'Look a little further along,' he pointed.

She put the book back and then realised she had been staring right at the book she was searching for. The library was the proud home of many complete sets of texts for studying the art of sorcery. She was taken aback by the sheer volume of what she was seeing. She followed the line around the corner to the next lot of shelves. It was amazing, how wiccan managed to get hold of it was another matter. 'How do I know which one to choose?'

'That's the complicated part, I am afraid we don't know,' he commented.

The sudden enthusiasm changed to a hint of annoyance, as she poked her head back around the corner to look at Jedd. She asked, 'Dare I ask the question; how do I find out?'

'Well it's like this…' Jedd began.

'You mean I need to find out on my own,' she sighed.

This was not going well, and Saranon found herself in one of those awkward situations. The two had meant well and to let a sorcerer in this far, by the looks of some of the startled people around her, was quite a privilege. She held back the words she wanted to say and gave herself a moment to relax. 'I'm grateful for you allowing me access' there was a small pause. 'I know it means a lot.'

Celia's face beamed, 'I knew you would understand.'

Saranon felt like someone had opened a big door then slammed it shut in her face. She held back how upset she was, but Jedd could see it in her eyes. Sorcery was a complicated art and learning from the wrong book could be worse than not having studied at all.

She let out a sigh of frustration and resigned herself to being back where she started. The place was a hive of activity and so she let Celia take the lead while her dreams went stale inside. If she could remember her parents she would have somewhere to start, her lack of knowledge would make it all the more difficult. At least there remained a little ray of hope, her experiences would help progress her down the right path only at a much slower pace. Bellington Castle was some way out of normal travel and it was soon growing dark. The skies greyed outside reflecting Saranon's sullen mood. Being amongst so many wiccan felt a little peculiar, but she was in the company of friends. In the small room she shared with Celia she soon fell asleep.

In the early hours of the dark her dreams twisted again from the normal nondescript into a transverse harsh reality. The hollow temple was behind her as she stood near the water's edge. It flowed down with a peaceful tranquillity and somehow she knew not to touch it. This time she followed the stream, and heard a voice behind her. Tasha smiled, which way are you going? Saranon replied, I don't know. Tasha stood beside her and answered, well you had better decide soon the water's getting cold. She looked back, and saw that the stream had begun to freeze. I need to leave, she was thinking of the fact that she had wasted time instead of heading straight to Serenphel. Tasha pointed ahead, no; you need to decide which path you are taking.

In the distance Saranon saw the path fork not once but many times over, travelling in different directions. Some wrapped around each other and others went past the way she came. She half expected Tasha to disappear, but her old friend was still there beside her. Saranon spoke in her dream, why are you helping me? Tasha responded; you are too valuable to us. Saranon smelled a rat, us, who are you? Tasha spoke; you know who we are you hear us calling. Saranon gasped, that's not possible. Deep down she knew, but she had thought it was all her imagination. After all no one else she had come across had admitted to hearing a Keep.

She woke in a cold sweat, Celia was sound asleep in the other bed, so she tried to manoeuvre out of the room. Between hitting her toe while finding her slippers and the creak of the door, she was relieved to see no sign of movement from Celia. She cringed as the old boards on the stairs creaked as she made her way down to the kitchen to get a glass of water. A small light had been left on and she made herself at home. Her ears pricked up as a whimpering sound behind her made her jump. She almost spilled the water and placed the jug down.

The terrified young girl did not speak. Saranon gave her a large glass, half filled with water, which Reida grasped in both hands. Jedd's cousin had bandages hidden underneath her nightie and it reminded her of when she was back at the camps. She failed to understand the reasoning behind such cruel acts. The girl crinkled her sleeve and used it to wipe her mouth. Reida pointed to her bond-breaker. Saranon not thinking anything of it, took the blade out and transformed it into the long sword.

The girl seemed mesmerised. Without uttering a sound Reida reached out and brushed her fingertips across the flat of the blade. The bond-breaker lit up underneath the girls touch. Reida spoke in a soft voice, 'Will I grow up to be like you some day?'

She held back a hint of sadness, 'I think you're special being who you are.'

Reida stepped back and said in a small voice, 'I have to go now.'

With that the girl scampered like a little mouse off into the darkness of the hall and out of sight.

Saranon was not scared of the dark, but it brought back bad memories. Bellington Castle was a peaceful place, but not for her. After all even Celia out of jest, had commented on how unusual it was for a sorcerer to be invited to Bellington Castle. As she walked along she glanced out the window. Her eye caught on a shimmering image of a figure, just noticeable in the landscape behind it. She touched the door handle and her senses prickled. Somehow, she knew not to open it and went back upstairs ducking under the warm covers.

In the morning over breakfast, she told Celia, who listened with serious interest. Her friend talked about the wards protecting the building from intruders. Either way whatever the thing had been, it did not sound friendly. It took a while for Celia to convince her to travel a short distance across the estate to see some of the wildlife. In the end she thought if no one else was worried, then perhaps it was best if she just went with the flow. The scenery was lush and green with plenty of colour from the flower gardens as they made their way into the woodland. It was polite to limit the use of sorcery here, as it could set off wards and traps that Saranon did not want to get tangled up in.

Celia had gone a little further and was almost hidden as she bent down to pick something up she cradled it in her arms. As she walked over, its tail bobbed beneath her forearm, 'Here you go.'

Celia announced as she handed over the creature into Saranon's arms. She was unprepared for the tiny creature. It looked like a miniature dragon that had crossed itself with a multi-coloured parrot. Its beak nuzzled into her arm as it tried to hide, its back legs managed to break free. With a clumsy start it half jumped, and flew away. She was amazed, 'What is it?'

'It's a palafon,' Celia pointed to some hiding in the trees.

They were strange creatures that were just as happy on the ground as in a tree. She had to be careful where she stepped as the little dragons loved hiding in leaves and anything else that lay scattered around. She tried to catch one, at the last minute it jolted and then ran off at a fast pace. Leaving Saranon wondering how Celia had managed to catch one at all. She soon resigned herself to the fact that they preferred to be looked at, as she sat down on the soft grass keeping still. Together they explored the rest of the estate while avoiding the workers and people who had come to study. It was a fine day with most of the occupants and visitors outdoors. Celia had introduced her to many, but she was not good with remembering names. She had the distinct feeling that by the time she left, everyone was going to know her.

In a well-worn field a couple of small groups were gathering and chopping wood. They built two large piles for the nights festivities. By the way Celia and Jedd liked partying it was an integral part of being wiccan. Saranon enjoyed the events because of the wonderful spread of food. At the tavern Mrs Harper and Celia made cooking look easy, but her attempts were rather dull in comparison. Coloured ribbons and cloth were being hung up on poles and nearby branches. Now that she knew what to look for, she noticed a palafon trying to tear a piece of ribbon out of a tree. Celia glanced at the scene and explained, 'They like the bright colours.'

Jedd was helping oversee the arrangements with his mother Emily. She was a beautiful lady with fine features that outshone her ordinary clothes. From what Saranon could hear she also had a decent set of lungs as her voice carried over the band as it practiced. Emily was in the middle of yelling out to two young men who had taken a heavy crate in the wrong direction. Jedd waved from a distance and Emily turned to meet them with a pleasant smile, 'Hello, have you two come to help?'

Before she could answer and say no, Emily butted in. 'There are piles of ribbons and banners over there, if you get started now we'll be finished on time.'

Celia grabbed her arm so they could escape anything else Emily might think of. She was hesitant since she had left the camps, she had no trouble saying no to people and did not like being told what to do. Celia saw the look on her face, 'Come on it'll be fun, besides its better than some of the other jobs she's asked me to do.'

Saranon was still moaning after they had made it to the bottom of the first box. She wondered how in the Zyanthian Region she had managed to find herself decorating. She hung up the colourful pieces of material. When she had left Darkonia, this had not exactly been at the top of her list of things to do.

Celia pranced around as though she had been given the best job in the world, twirling around on her toes as she went. She wondered if this was the real reason why sorcerers rarely came to Bellington Castle. So they could avoid the boring and onerous task of decorating. She was trying hard to remain polite about the whole situation, when a third box was carted along and dumped near the second. She thought to herself, yes this was definitely the reason why sorcerers stayed away. An elderly lady called out to let them know it was afternoon tea. Both girls ran off to the tent where a wonderful array of smells, from fresh baked cakes met them.

Their task was finished and as Emily had predicted, just in time. They rushed back to their rooms to rest a moment before changing. Saranon was not into bright coloured clothing and had to be convinced to wear something different. In the end she settled for somewhere halfway. As the two of them made their way down the stairs, they encountered several performers all made up. She and Celia had to make their way through the maze and out to the fresh air, as the day was turning to dusk. The bonfires in the distance had been lit and the flames were starting to reach their height. The first band for the evening was getting ready. The two girls joined the growing formation of colourful outfits down on the grassy slope. Jedd managed to find them through the crowd and led them over to a good spot, close to the band and the food.

CHAPTER NINE

Celebrating at Bellington Castle

It was difficult to hear over the loud music and Saranon followed Celia's lead toward the outer ring of people to get some fresh air. They both lay down in a crumpled heap, as Celia stretched her arms and legs out in a butterfly motion. Saranon asked 'Does this happen at the end of every week?'

Celia cracked up laughing through her dry voice, 'No, just four times a year at each equinox and solstice. When you return you'll know where to find us.'

She was pondering whether this was good or bad when she could sense Jedd running towards them from the direction of the castle. At first she ignored it, but he seemed to be running fast. She began to get up and Celia saw her puzzled stare. She could see Jedd coming towards them, he plunged down and grabbed Saranon by the arm. She almost toppled to the ground trying to find her step. Without stopping he spoke, 'You have to come, it's important.'

Celia did not want to be left behind and was determined to follow. She became serious, 'What's going on?'

'You have to see,' Jedd answered.

They dashed in a clumsy fashion through the inner courtyard, bypassing a couple of serious figures to enter the main hall. Celia ran in ahead, her shoes crunched the scatterings of shattered glass. Before they had time to enter, the colour had slid out of her cheeks as she let out a gasp. Saranon entered, there were spots of blood on the floor, most of it had missed the rugs.

The cabinet had been broken into, with several objects missing that she had seen when she first came. She walked up and touched the back of the cabinet. It was enough to give her a vague impression of what had happened. She crossed over to the door and walked out into the dark night air. It had been a wonderful evening where, for a while, she had forgotten what she was, but this had brought her slamming back down to reality. Away from the castle she could raise her energy, without setting off the warning systems which protected the place. The fact that these had not worked, made Saranon worry even more, she was beginning to feel uneasy as she ran further away from the castle.

She walked through the scrub with ease, using her energy to quicken her pace. During her stay in Alveron she had learned to hide herself well. A basic process, yet she had much to catch up on. Further ahead she could sense wiccan, but that did not make sense. The prized artefacts had been well protected and wiccan would have detected their own. She crouched as she came closer to where two men and a young boy had taken a moment to rest. The two men were arguing and the bag holding their stolen booty had been left unattended. She thought that it was all too easy and stayed back.

Sitting on the cold ground in the dark she listened to the voices of the two men.

'If Lord Karager finds out we're involved, our clan will be done for.'

'He won't, not with a break in like that. He'll suspect the wizards like old Damon said.'

Saranon had heard about old Damon as he was referred to. In actual fact Damon was not that old. He came from a long line of leaders from the sorcerer community and should not be encouraging the theft of artefacts. She unsheathed her bond-breaker and transformed in silence. She used the dagger to take a peek inside the bag, and found what she suspected a tracking device.

She had little time and used some of the trinkets she had gathered to fill the bag, after she had lifted the artefacts out. As she headed away, she could sense a sorcerer approaching and went into full flight using her energy to run faster. She could feel the panic rise in her chest and before she could think, she saw someone up ahead. She slowed down, but not enough to avoid crashing into Jedd near the perimeter, her heart was still racing fast as they went inside. Lord Karager was waiting with several wiccan talking in hushed voices, which ceased as they entered the room. The artefacts were taken away for safekeeping. The shock of what had happened was still sinking in.

Lord Karager turned to face Saranon, 'You have done us a great service. I ask that you not speak of this again.'

'Damon was trying to set you up,' she blurted out in a rush.

'We know, this is something we must deal with,' he responded.

Even though Lord Karager spoke with a soft tone, his words resonated with strength. It left her in no doubt that he was not one to be crossed. In that moment she felt as though she had just been sidelined and her small triumph meant nothing. Yet this was not her world and she did not want to create problems. She left the small group behind. When she went upstairs she found Celia already asleep, she sat on the bed in the dark and stared out the window. Her head was still churning with the chase and it gave her an uneasy feeling that would not settle.

The sound of the night's activities crept in through the cracks around the glass in the window. Saranon decided that it was a good thing she had not encountered the sorcerer community before. Whatever it was they were up to she did not want to be caught in the middle. As she curled up in bed the events still haunted her. She lay awake for a while before her tired eyes closed, marking the start of a heavy sleep. The morning was a little cool as she and Celia got dressed and raced down the stairs to breakfast.

Unfortunately, they could hear Emily in the background looking for volunteers to clean up. The two sat near a corner so as not to be noticed through the doorway. This was a challenge in itself, as everybody else had the same idea.

As much as Saranon had loved the celebrations of last night, she was itching to have another look at the library. Celia had more important things to do like catch up with her friends. So she found herself in the midst of some peculiar sets of books. Along the way she had picked up a few tricks and now was a perfect time to test one out. It would take her too long to read every single book, even if she managed to copy them. She pulled out a few trinkets from Odana they were small and handy for transferring knowledge. Not quite as complex as a talik, but it would do what Saranon wanted. She glanced over her shoulder, there were a few people in the library, though no one was paying attention to her.

She picked up the first book and held it as though she was reading it. She held the device out, it was a simple transfer of knowledge to the device. If she went through all the books the compounding effect would make her drowsy. After last night it could be considered normal. The task filled the day, though it was better than expected. She had found something which excited her senses, a small set of books which had been tucked away near the top of the shelf. It was a full set of the Uvalen Code, a complex masterpiece describing the natural laws that governed sorcery. As Saranon slept that night she concentrated on that part, at first the text was rather strange, but it started to unravel.

The last few days she lay low, she had taken on too much, even though at the time she thought she could manage it. The result was that she looked unwell and did not stray too far. She was resting on a wooden deck chair when the Lord met her for the second time, 'Did you find what you were looking for?'

Lord Karager for all his harsh edges and large stance was a strange and elegant man, who showed the signs of a worried father. Saranon could not help feeling sorry for him, 'Yes.'

'You realise that one day you will wake up and all our struggles will seem insignificant.'

She knew what he meant, it was unusual for a sorceress to have so much to do with wiccan, 'I'm not so sure.'

'Just remember when that day comes, we will understand,' he spoke with a hint of kindness in his voice.

Saranon did not want to think of a time when that would happen and she hoped the Lord was not right. As Lord Karager left, his words gave rise to more unanswered questions for her to think about, but for now she would enjoy the time she had.

The journey was over far too soon as she and Celia packed for the trip back. 'Did coming here help?' Celia enquired.

'I think it did,' she replied.

'What will you do when we return?' Celia asked.

'Oh, I don't know I thought a tavern might be a nice

place to stay.'

Celia looked up at her and smiled, 'You mean you like mother's cooking.'

'That too,' she added.

Jedd joined them on the trip back he wanted to talk about what had happened, but held back. The great Bellington Castle faded in the distance and Saranon felt like there was something she needed to do before she left. The Keeps were trying to communicate with her and she wanted to know why. The strange dream had returned to haunt her through everything else and she wanted to get to bottom of it, before it became too weird. This meant spending more time in Redadere. She had made good time from Alveron and she wanted to make the most of her travels. Their arrival was late, but the fires were still keeping the tavern warm, which took the chill away from their cloaks.

As Saranon took off her cloak, she peered out the window, for a moment she could have sworn she saw the fuzzy outline of a figure, then it vanished. Celia had not thought anything about her last sighting, so she chose not to mention it. It was not long before she made her way upstairs. She was in the middle of getting ready for bed, when she had a change of heart and decided to take a look outside. The night air was sharp and crisp, but she was well dressed, this time she was ready for a chase. It was difficult, though she managed to find a glimpse of the silhouette. At this stage she was not sure if it was the same one, but she continued anyway.

She kept to the background, the figure was making its way back to Greddin Fort. The place had been built as a fortress. Only half way through someone had changed the plans, or at least that was what it looked like. For some strange reason the two designs worked and gave the Keep an imposing stature. The outer rim of the Keep was not a problem for her and she followed at a distance, just before the doorway the figure materialised. It was a wizard, which made sense, a wizard would not raise much alarm at Bellington Castle since there they were not a real threat. She was about to leave when the voice in her dreams revealed itself, come in. It was the Keep, but then Greddin was quite powerful and this was who she had wanted to meet.

Saranon chose to go in through a more discreet entrance around the corner, it led down. She had seen quite a few Keeps up close and this did not faze her. She made her way below the hustle and bustle that dripped snippets of noise down the large vents. She was looking at the indolin chambers which sat below the last part of the habitable area of the Keep. She placed her hand on the wall to try and find an entrance. A small seal lit up near her hand, identifying the area where she was, as part of the chambers opened up. She stood back unsure, and the Keep called, you are here.

Something was wrong, the place was almost lifeless. This should have been the busiest and most vibrant area, a place where the Keep could be itself with little interference. Saranon had done repair work before, and Keeps were not new to her so she took the opportunity to look around. At a glance it was not immediately obvious though she had seen this sort of thing before, so it was not a deterrent. She was going to find out what was going on, it would mean having to get dirty. She made a start in the dim areas taking down notes and measurements. It was a wonder no one above her had noticed, then stranger things happened.

Saranon had set herself a small task to begin with, but by the time she had been around the main area it had taken a while. Outside was still dark and she managed to slip out unnoticed back into a safe warm bed. The night's adventures had left her with a lot to think about, why would wizards be keeping a distant eye on her, at least she assumed it was her. The weather had turned outside into a dismal rain which darkened the day, now that she knew what to look for spotting the wizards was easy. During the day they tried to blend in rather than disappear. She had a list of things to get and Jedd had helped to point her in the right direction. At least with asking wiccan she would not raise any suspicions about what she was up to. The inner workings of the Keep were knowledge more likely to be held by wizards or sorcerers than anyone else.

The difficult part though would be making the tools, the process would be more obvious. Jedd's friend was an apprentice blacksmith who could provide a suitable location. It would be less noticeable since the kedrils looked somewhat similar. The Keep Greddin had been kind enough to pass on the information she needed, as each Keep was different. The workshop was a simple and grubby place, but Saranon had grown up in squalor so she felt quite at home. She set to work with the experience of someone who had made specialised tools for a Keep before. She was not good at making normal tools, but a kedril was a fine work of art, even if the finished product did not look as dainty.

Normal tools as she had found out were nowhere near as good when repairing a Keep. Celia who had become interested, set to work making a special leather carry bag. Most Keeps had their own kedrils which were tucked away in easy to find places often by the inhabitants. Yet as she had found out, Greddin had spoken the truth when he said there were none in the chambers. Saranon was a quick worker and made good progress, but there was still some work left to do. She stopped early in the afternoon, something had been bothering her, like a niggling feeling at the back of her neck. She packed up leaving the place as she had found it and searched around to find out what was causing her senses to go funny.

As she walked along the streets she could feel herself starting to slip into a trance like state, and tried to keep on the verge of falling in. Whatever it was, it had to be getting close, she placed her hand on Tellembre, it was warm with excitement. It knew what was going on before she did. Her senses intensified until she could work out what was going on and where. Saranon was heading towards the factories. To where a large old building lay hidden among the grimy structures. As she drew closer she slid near the edges, she could spot some wizards close by, they appeared to be here for the same reason she was. She could not find an entrance without being seen. Walls were not a problem as she had discovered earlier and placed her hand up to the brickwork.

There was enough leeway to allow her to go through unnoticed as she took a moment to calm herself. Inside she was in control, but that could change, and she did not know how long it would take. With no further thought she entered, unaware that a small edge of her robe, the last to go through had been seen by one of the wizards. The wizard rushed to enter the same way to no avail the wall was thick and Saranon was oblivious to what had just happened. Inside the story become clear, the wizards had been trying to deal with a group of dark sorcerers who had made this their den. She crept along trying to follow glimpses of movement out of the corner of her eye. This required concentration, in the space of a heart beat she felt herself slip and managed to regain control.

There were noises up ahead and she ran through a large room. Before she could make it back toward the door, a large strong arm, dripping sweat and holding a bond-breaker lunged around her head. She managed to duck around taking hold of the wizard's arm and sensed a sorceress to the left. She shoved the wizard's bond-breaker into the sorceress with the momentum of his own swing. The dagger pierced the sorceress wounding her in the stomach and she vanished from sight. The wizard did not look impressed.

Saranon turned to run and standing on the other side of the doorway were two of the wizards companions, they ran towards her. She sensed two more sorcerers. Before the wizards were able to enter the room, she had reached for both her bond-breakers, Tellembre and Corsavere. She drew them at full length. She used them to plunge deep into the sorcerers by each side. Her hands with the bond-breakers outstretched. Both sorcerers revealed themselves to the naked eye before falling on the floor, both dead.

All three wizards stopped in shock, Saranon took the advantage and ran after the wounded sorceress. As she ran she could hold on no longer and transformed into the Angeon only this time, she knew something was different. She felt in control, or at least she thought she did. Her senses lived for the chase and in this form the wounded sorceress was not hard to find. She had put Corsavere back in its hiding place. It was a strange bond-breaker even to its creator. She was more familiar with Tellembre. The chase made her feel alive and even though she had more control this time, she did not feel like herself. It was as though she were looking through someone else's eyes. The sorceress was slowing down up ahead from the injury, Saranon approached her near the end of the alley.

The sorceress looked up knowing what she saw and what was to come. She did not resist as Saranon placed her left hand on the lady's head. She looked up at Saranon, 'You feel it too, it's only a matter of time. You will be like us,' the lady spoke.

Saranon let the sorceress's life drain from her in a quiet peaceful death. As soon as the last breath was taken the horrible marks that showed the path she had been chosen appeared over her body. The once elegant lady now looked haggard and ugly. She left unnoticed and did not feel any sense of empathy for the lady. Her choice in life had been made long before Saranon had set foot on Normisian soil.

As she transformed back, she wondered who was her real self, the one she had grown up with, or the new one she was yet to know. Either way something had changed. She felt a sense of satisfaction at her achievement. At the same time she was worried that she had just opened a door that could not be closed again. Her endeavours had taken her long enough. She forgot about the wizards as she went back to the tavern for a hardy meal and a good night's sleep. As she trundled off to sleep, the events of the evening gripped her in a strange nightmare that made her sweat.

In her dream she was running through the building, the sorcerers were still there and she was running to find someone. She went down in the basement, there was a locked door blocking her way she pelted herself against the door and it gave with a rush. There was blood on the floor and she saw Tasha's body as she had found it at Antavagon. Saranon jolted awake with a start, it was still dark outside, but she could not get back to sleep. She threw back the covers and started downstairs. At the top of the balustrade she could hear Mrs Harper speaking with a few of the older wiccan and stopped to listen.

They were talking about what had happened. Though from what she could make out, this time they did not know that she had helped. She decided it was safer to go back to her room. She opened the window and looked out on the world below. Sure enough she saw a strange outline of a figure across the road. She looked straight at it, but the blur hurt her eyes. She stayed sitting on the sill of the large window, which doubled as a door, until her eyes grew tired with sleep and she returned to bed. The rain had decided to make another morning miserable as Saranon made her way to the workshop. She was pleased with her work and lost track of everything else around her, while she concentrated on her goal.

The kedrils were easy for her to make, but for anyone else it would have taken longer. She had finished just after lunch, there were only a few. The small group did not look like much, but they were well designed for the task at hand. Celia had finished the case the night before and she placed them in with care as she cleaned up. Saranon headed off towards Greddin Fort. It was easier to go in the back-way near the dragons, she was less likely to be noticed. With a thought she changed the look of her clothes to blend in. There was a lot of activity around her, which was a good distraction, as she slipped past. She was about to open a concealed door, when she heard screams and shouting coming from inside the dragon pens.

At first she was going to ignore it, but the commotion was getting more serious. She stopped short of the entrance knowing that she would regret intervening. She flung herself into the situation with such determination that no one questioned why she was there. The stench of dragon's blood was sickening. One of the large males with a name tag hanging around its neck that said 'Splodge' had panicked. The dragon had wounded himself against some armoury, with two spears sticking out of his behind. One of the trainers who had been injured was trying to lie still on the floor. While several others not so experienced, were trying to calm the dragon. The great beast was stopping them from getting to the trainer.

It was an awful mess and before Saranon could do anything, someone else had been hurt by the dragon. Splodge was heightening into a mad panic. The dragon managed to storm past the first group of people, straight into her path. She held up her right hand, and touched the magnificent creature on the nose. It let out a low squeak that sounded like a sigh of relief then dropped its head and lowered it by her side. Another trainer who had arrived pulled out the spears. The dragon hardly noticed as its breathing started to return to normal. While the place was still a buzz with excitement and fear, she crept away hoping that no one would notice she was not supposed to be there.

CHAPTER TEN

An untidy welcome to Greddin Fort

As Saranon closed the door behind her she heard a man call out. 'Hey, where did that girl go?'

She cringed, and cursed her good nature. It was going to land her in trouble again, but she had plenty of time to think about that later. The Keep was relieved to have her back. The indolin chambers were calm and peaceful. This time she travelled down to take a closer look, it was not difficult to figure out where to go. The skada were the mechanical creatures that helped to repair the Keep. They had the misfortune of looking like large spiders and were leaving an obvious trail to follow. The problem with skada was their limitations. They were not smart and if anything major happened, they were not equipped to cope.

Saranon made her way trying not to tread on the creatures as they scuttled down the hall way. One she just missed it made some sort of angry gesture before carrying on its way. To her they were like living creatures with their own personalities made by the Keep. As she came to the end of the line she peered through to one of the substations that looked after a large section of the habitable areas. There were small signs of damage and she said out loud, 'It doesn't look that bad.'

One of the skada near her feet started jumping up and down tugging at the end of her trousers. She followed the little creature around the substation to where the engines were, that ran it. She peered down into the darkness in the opening to a large room. As she made out what was below she gasped. Two of the cylinders looked like ants nests from a distance, there were skada swarming all over them. Something had gone through the system that had made a giant mess.

Saranon looked at the skada that had climbed up on the rail looking for some sign that this could be fixed. The skada held its front legs together in a gesture that looked like it was expecting her to come up with a plan. No wonder she had not found any kedrils in the chambers, all of them would be in use on a job of this scale. the only entity big enough to fix this was the Keep itself. To do that the entire substation would need to be placed out of action. It was no small task, but delaying it would make the Keep more vulnerable.

All of a sudden her little repair job just got a whole lot bigger. She let out a moan of disbelief and the skada scuttled after her as she went. She stopped and kneeled down, 'I'm afraid I will have to tackle this from the other end. I am going to have to go up and change the system over to compensate for when this one goes offline.'

The skada hugged Saranon's leg, then wandered off back to work. She felt sorry for the poor creatures, but she had to leave and go upward. There were hallways that led up, but this would mean going through someone else's basement. The thought did not appeal to her. She did not want to go looking through other people's dirty laundry.

It was getting near tea time and if she did not return, Mrs Harper who had become quite fond of her, would wonder where she was. The pathway was clear and Saranon slipped out of the Keep unnoticed. When she reached the tavern she heard a few of the patrons mentioning what had happened at Greddin. Celia found her, 'Did you hear about all the excitement at Greddin Fort, a girl saved the life of a dragon trainer.'

Celia eyed her with suspicion, she did not know what to say. 'I thought it was you,' Celia whispered. 'There aren't many girls that can subdue one of Greddin's most prized dragons.'

Saranon wondered how the dragon had gotten the name Splodge and if that was important. It did not sound regal. 'Splodge?' She asked.

'Yes he was hand raised from a hatchling,' Celia explained.

She found it difficult to believe a creature that size had ever been small and with that thought, the two sat down for tea. She stayed up searching through her hand written notes and a few manuals she had found at Bellington Castle. The problem at Greddin ate away at her.

Now that she knew what was wrong, her mind was busy working on a solution. The end of the week festivities were finding their way through the floorboards to upstairs. Celia knocked on the door while Saranon packed her scribbles away and followed her friend downstairs. If there was one thing she could rely on the Harper's knew how to unwind. The music relieved her of her problems and that of the Keep. The air was getting hot inside and she went out onto the street where a few of the patrons had already gathered.

The night was cool and two of the patrons nearby had just decided to get into an argument over who had bumped who first. It was starting to get too noisy and ending up in a brawl was not her idea of fun, so she went for a stroll further up the street. She could hear the start of some heavy punching and Mrs Harper's voice ringing out behind her. It was calm and peaceful, a good night for thinking of how she was going to help the Keep. She looked up at the stars, and felt a strong breeze beside her, she thought it was odd. Two big sweaty arms gripped her and pulled her around the corner toward a waiting cart. Saranon tried to pull herself free, but this time she had been caught unaware. She kicked at the wizard as another hauled her inside, pinning her to the ground.

She knew they were blocking her cries from being heard by passers-by. She did not feel like crying, she just wanted to shout with anger and since she knew they could hear her she did not hold back. The wizard who had grabbed her blocked her in and her short temper was starting to fray at the edges. After being stuck in the camps a few wizards did not scare her as much as it might have. She could hear Celia calling out in the distance, on the floor near her she saw the emblem of the army on the cloak of one of the wizards. The men and one lady acted as though this was a normal everyday occurrence. The cart made a tight bend around a corner with the jerk of the moving wheels Saranon leaped and managed to jump free. Tumbling out, she ran down a side street, and used her sorcery to blend into the background.

The small group hardly made a sound, but she knew they were there and that they would know what to look for. Running with the wizards close by, could mean being found so she stayed put. She could hear the footsteps of the lady nearby then they faded. She waited through the night keeping awake. The sun was well in the sky and she had not heard any sign of the wizards for hours. Saranon made a move to stand up. Mitch who had been waiting, tackled her to the ground. He held her hands behind her. She was not impressed and for the second time she was bundled into the cart. This time she had to endure the bumpy ride all the way back to Greddin Fort, this was not part of her plan.

She could feel herself starting to heat up from the anger as she was shoved inside. Mitch kept her close, not wanting to make the same mistake twice, as the door closed behind them, Saranon could feel the wizards relax. The people around her looked as though they were used to seeing someone in her position making a lot of commotion. This time they would be disappointed. She was already assessing the surroundings planning a possible way of getting out. She was so silent that the rest of the party almost forgot she was there, after the language she had used in the cart. She was taken down to one of the holding cells, which looked familiar from her days in the camp.

Saranon was not the only one down there, an older sorceress had the cell opposite. 'We told you, you would join us,' the dark sorceress spoke with confidence.

She realised what she had been placed near, she examined the bars to no avail. 'You know it's too late,' the dark sorceress spoke.

Saranon turned and looked at the lady, but said nothing. Her only saving grace was that she had managed to save Tellembre which she often wore out in the open. Though sometimes she thought the bond-breaker had a mind of its own, either way she was not going to let the thing next to her know what she had. She was starting to wonder why she had been brought here, when there was a movement near the door. A more sinister wizard in long dark robes entered with two guards.

They approached Saranon and removed her from the cell, all the while she remained silent, like when she had been in the camps. They cuffed her hands and moved her forward as she was taken down to a lower level. She wondered if this was how Tasha had felt. The guards took her into a grimy room and made her kneel on the floor, one of them holding her head down. She could make out from the corner of her eye the one with the dark robes heading toward her holding something with a tool. He approached her and a searing pain etched through her skin as the wizard placed the thing around her neck. She did not move and she did not scream instead, she seethed in silent anger. They would pay she would make them pay.

The guard released the cuffs from around her hands and she felt sick, sick with anger and pain. The guards took her back to the cell, where the dark sorceress, Chevonne watched in fascination. Saranon noticed that the lady was wearing the same device. When the guards left the lady smiled, 'You will be like us soon.'

Saranon felt the device and she knew what it was, but she did not give any sign of recognition. One of the hazards of her previous life meant knowing too much about what sort of devices could be used against her. She had been foolish to think the wizards, or the army for that matter, would not resort to such tactics. The rest of the day went slow with her temper simmering underneath the surface.

As the light from the early dusk spread up the wall, the sounds of a commotion reached the cells. The dark sorceress next to her sat calm, Saranon could sense that the lady knew what was going on. The sounds outside went silent as her heart skipped a beat. When Chevonne's companions glided between the cells, Saranon hoped they would leave her, but they opened both cells. Chevonne laughed as they took Saranon out into the depths of the Keep. She tried to avoid being touched by the tainted sorcerers, but that seemed to make it worse as they held her so she could not get away.

The guards looked as though they had not stood a chance. She was led through a rabbit warren of corridors, before they entered a large open area. She could hear the sound of more tainted sorcerers before she saw them. One of them had a tool which removed the device from around Chevonne's neck, she turned to Saranon, 'Now you will become like us.'

She was shoved in the middle, as the sorcerers formed a circle around her trapping her in the centre. From outside the circle she saw real trouble heading her way, the head of the group was coming to complete the circle. Saranon concentrated as much as she could, but the device around her neck was holding her back.

Cornell approached without haste. This was not something that needed to be rushed. Saranon prepared herself, but it would not be enough. It was the best she could do and she needed to feel that she could do something. As Cornell joined the circle she gulped, this was not what she had planned. The first wave knocked her to the ground, she had to fight to resist the pull against her. Even if it tore her apart inside, she thought that would be a better solution and wondered if Tasha had made the same choice. The wave almost crushed her to the ground, but she managed to hold on, she had to hold on. The circle was closing in and she would have to try something to break their sorcery.

Saranon's breath was burning through her lungs and

she realised she was heating up. Sweat poured down her forehead and onto her cheeks. She looked down and saw charred remnants. It was all that was left of the device around her neck. She looked up no one had noticed, they were too busy satisfying their own means. The circle of sorcerers came ever closer and she could see the start of the third wave pummelling towards her in flecks of light. In that moment she stood up and reached out with her sorcery hurling the intensity of her energy out into the group. The explosion of the raging force fell almost all the members of the circle, except one.

Cornell opened up his arms as the wave of sorcery flared and aimed for Saranon with an immense force. She had time to see it coming and braced herself ready for the impact. Out of the corner of her eye she could see Mitch, running full pelt toward Cornell. Just before impact the wizard, Mitch took part of the blow. He managed to ram his bond-breaker home in the sorcerer's ribs before his injured body dropped to the ground. She could do nothing as she watched on helplessly. All she could do was try to block as much of the attack as possible, but the damage was already done.

Saranon held on under the strain as Cornell continued his attack, but as much as he tried to hide it, the injury had taken its toll. She held on as she summoned every last bit of her strength and hurled it with a renewed determination. The blow struck true as Cornell winced and fell to his knees on the floor. For a moment he waved his hands and she braced herself for another attack. Then without any warning he collapsed as the last breath left his body. She remained still, not ready to believe it was over. Yet as she waited she could sense that it was over, as she stood in open astonishment. Her body ached as she walked over to Mitch who was lying still, he was breathing which was a good sign.

Saranon opened one of her sova bags and took out a compact tray which folded out to be large enough to hold the weight of a person. She lifted Mitch up and floated the tray at waist height. He was still awake, but he was in no shape to argue. She took one last look to make sure Cornell was dead and knelt down to pick up the charred remnants of the device. When she got hold of that wizard, she would have a few choice things to say. So as not to make Mitch uncomfortable she pulled the tray along at a slow pace. She was not sure where to go and the Keep was being unhelpful. She did not blame him, but someone had to be at the other end giving orders. She could hear Mitch's laboured breathing and moved ahead with a sense of urgency in her step.

Unfortunately without the Keep's help, the place was difficult to navigate. At one stage she managed to get herself completely lost, until she found the trail of markers again above the doors. Saranon took a path which she thought would lead to the medical area, but she was not one hundred percent sure. She finally opened a door that led into the hub of human life, with people coming and going. She took a quick glance to see if any were from the army. If they were she could not see any sign and decided to take a risk. A lady approached her and asked her what she was doing. She thought that was obvious then answered and the lady went off to get someone.

While Saranon was waiting, she could tell Mitch was trying to say something, so she leaned closer. 'You need to go there,' Mitch managed to point to a corridor.

She was not going to stay and find out what was going on, especially as the only reason she had come was to help him. So she took off down the path that he had pointed out. As they were going she spotted the marks above the door that she had been looking for. From there made it to the medical area within the Keep. She slowed down as she entered the foyer and realised that Mitch was not the only one who had been hurt. Around her she could see other casualties waiting for treatment.

Saranon could see a lady by the name of Rachel in the middle of a conversation with the man at the front desk. Rachel looked up a little puzzled at the sight of her with Mitch and hurried the two in so that he could be examined. She waited on one of the benches as Rachel called over one of the doctors to look at Mitch. They were clouding their words so that she could not ease drop. She could tell by their tones that his condition was serious. She felt a bit small and useless. A lot had happened in a small amount of time and her mind was still trying to catch up. She was grateful for what Mitch had done, even if he had not intended to help save her. If he had not intervened Saranon was not sure if she could have dealt with Cornell on her own.

She did not like to admit it, but she owed him a great deal for what he had done. Even though she was sitting out of the way, she could tell people around her were staring at her and was yet to find out why she had been targeted. This combined with the attack inside the Keep gave an uneasy feel to the place and everyone seemed to be at the end of their nerves. The second doctor wheeled Mitch away, he was deteriorating fast and was almost conscious. Saranon wondered if her help would be in vain. Rachel brought her a drink and sat beside her. Rachel seemed nice enough, so she explained what had happened. She neglected to mention the part about the restraint that had been placed around her neck. She did not want to discuss that.

Rachel listened with sympathy, 'Do you know why the army is interested in you?'

She gave an honest answer, 'No.'

'So you don't know anything that could have attracted their attention?'

'I have difficulty blending in, I just don't know,' she exclaimed.

'It's okay. I know you are concerned for Mitch, you are welcome to wait here while he's in surgery.'

Saranon was shocked to hear the reality of how bad it was, 'Is he going to be okay?'

'I've seen Mitch survive worse,' Rachel answered.

Captain Mirshendy entered with a couple of officers. Rachel touched his arm on the way through and pulled him to the side, 'Are you missing a sorceress?'

The Captain spoke as he peered over her shoulder,

'You know I am.'

'She's not going anywhere,' Rachel replied.

The Captain looked confused and Rachel continued, 'She's attached to Mitch.'

'I have to deal with her,' the Captain spoke.

'I said she's attached to Mitch,' Rachel responded.

The realisation of what Rachel was saying started to show on the Captain's face, 'Do you mean to tell me?'

'Yes Jerald, that's exactly what I mean,' Rachel answered.

Saranon looked on, reading only their body language as the words remained muffled and she let out a frustrated sigh.

For a brief moment she locked eyes with the Captain and wondered if he had been the source of her trouble. She dangled the charred remnants of the hyrik that had been around her neck, catching his attention. He watched transfixed then without any hint of what he was thinking turned to leave. Rachel gave her an unimpressed glance before taking the object away. The lack of the hyrik did not seem to bother Rachel, yet Saranon had the feeling that did not matter. She could sense Rachel's energy, and was not about to annoy her.

CHAPTER ELEVEN

The help of a wizard

Saranon opened her eyes, and realised she was not at Mrs Harpers. The events of last night had left her feeling drained. The noise outside the room indicated that she had slept in she hurried herself to get ready and clambered out in a rush. She went over to the tea room. Rachel was there with a covered tray of breakfast for her. She rushed in, 'Sorry I'm late.'

'You are not late for anything. When you've finished Mitch asked for you.'

'He's okay?' Saranon spoke between mouthfuls.

'Yes,' Rachel replied.

She felt a little odd this morning, but she put that down to the attack last night. She wanted to make sure Mitch was all right before she left. Yet being at Greddin Fort presented itself with the potential to help the Keep, she would have to think about that. Mitch was awake in a room by himself. Saranon poked her head through the open door and he stared back, 'Is it all right…?'

'Yes,' he replied.

Saranon went with caution taking a good look to see if Mitch was okay and sat down next to the bed. Even lying down he was a big man. She looked at him and said, 'Thanks for helping me.'

Mitch did not answer instead he held her hand, the touch was strange and she realised what had happened. She felt sick, 'I'm sorry.' She stood up not knowing what to do, 'I'm sorry.'

Saranon held her hand to her mouth and turned to leave. Mitch spoke in a calm voice, 'Does this mean it was a mistake?'

She had to think about what she remembered on the subject, and what had happened, 'No it wasn't. I'm just sorry.'

She knew that to bond without good reason could be viewed as a great insult. She sat back down, 'I'm just sorry it had to be like that. I'm not sorry about the bond.'

'Now you're lying,' he replied.

'No. We haven't been bonded for long so you can't make that judgement yet,' she said with care.

'So now you're an expert,' he exclaimed.

'I didn't say that. I meant I did not expect to need the help of a wizard,' she was fumbling for words.

Mitch laughed, 'That's the first honest thing you've said.'

He raised himself on the pillow to sit up, 'How about we both keep quiet?'

'I can live with that,' she responded.

'Good, now are you going to hand that bond-breaker over to the army?'

'The bond hasn't sunk in yet has it?' She took the dagger out of its sheath so that Mitch could take a closer look.

He stared down at the hilt as he held it, 'That's less than six months old.'

'That's because I made it, it stays with me. No offence, but I don't part with that one,' she remarked.

Mitch handed it back, 'You are different to what I thought.'

'I hope that means I'm nicer!' Saranon was joking, but Mitch gave her a serious look.

She found the whole situation a bit awkward, but Mitch appeared to be taking it in his stride. Saranon cringed as he started describing a ceremony that would take place. It was beginning to sound like the bond was going to be more trouble than she expected. He held out his hand to comfort her, it was strange considering not long ago he had been trying to restrain her. She had not been involved in any wizard formalities and had tried to avoid them in Alveron. The little rituals were quite foreign to her and it had been easier to keep well clear.

She leaned over and placed her head on the bed trying to think of a way to get out of the ceremony. Yet she did not think that would be an option. Mitch looked up at the doorway and she could sense another wizard behind her. Captain Mirshendy was a little older than Mitch, who was only twenty-two. She found herself caught between focusing all her grievances on this man and seeing him as Mitch's old friend. She still held Mitch's hand as she sized up the Captain with an unimpressed glare. The Captain smiled, Rachel had been right, Saranon had become close to Mitch which could be used to their advantage.

She was not one to hide how she was feeling, 'What do you want?'

Captain Mirshendy walked over to them, 'I would like you to come for walk with me.'

She clenched Mitch's hand tighter and he broke the silence, 'I think you should go.'

She was not fond of being ordered about and she had not yet come to grips with the extent of her new responsibility. Yet the Captain may be able to answer some of her questions. She found herself in an uneasy situation as she followed him out to one of the small courtyards.

She took a quick glance around then turned back to face the Captain. 'Explain to me why I should not despise you for what you have done.'

Captain Mirshendy said nothing, so Saranon continued. 'If you had not brought me here none of this would have happened, or was that what you wanted?'

The Captain sat down so she did the same. She caught an insight to his thoughts, 'You only tolerate me because someone else does.'

The Captain showed no expression. She hung her

head with the thought, 'So where does that leave me?'

The Captain spoke, 'You pose a risk to us all. You cannot control yourself and you will spiral out of control unless something is done. In the mean time you will stay here.'

Saranon did not like that idea, but it would have to do since it would not raise suspicions while she assisted the Keep.

Her distain showed on her face, but she had to meet a compromise. 'Until you can prove that anything you just said is true, you don't lay a finger on me.'

Captain Mirshendy was not looking impressed, but she took no notice and walked off. Unfortunately Mitch was going to be bed bound for at least a few days and then there would be that annoying ceremony. Saranon found herself contemplating her next moves, while lying down in a large beautiful courtyard filled with a vibrant garden.

Its only misgivings were that the Captain, along with his comrades, had almost unlimited views of the entire area. The Tea Gardens as they were called, served a different purpose for her. It included several areas for easy access to the main workings of the Keep. She lay down staring at a little conduit which led up to a screen hidden amongst the bushes. She could hear a familiar clomping sound behind her. The Captain sat down beside her, 'You know everyone can see you through there.'

He pointed to a shiny black surface that covered the horizontal length of the wall. His body language was too hard to read. So she replied with a hint of sarcasm. 'There are more important things to worry about than wizards who enjoy interrupting my thinking time.'

The Captain started playing with the screen to her horror, 'Don't lose my work that took me ages.'

She was reminded yet again of all the reasons why wizards were annoying. As the Captain managed to flick through some of the readings for the vital areas of the Keep, before she closed it down. The two stared at each other in annoyance before the Captain broke first and asked Saranon to come inside. As she entered the inner stronghold it dawned on her just how alone she was. Everyone else seemed to fit into to a large group that sprang out of nowhere and she was left by herself. The Captain kept her close by, but she was intent on looking around. He sat her down next to Lyn, who did not look impressed. She was not sure whether she was on the verge of getting into trouble, or if the Captain was being polite. Either way it was hard to tell.

Captain Mirshendy opened up a large screen that came to lie along the length of the table. While Lyn exclaimed, 'Now I don't think that's a good idea.'

The Captain took no notice and changed the screen to reveal the blueprints in front of her. She was used to seeing Keeps in a different manner, so it took her a while to work out what was what, before making several variations. Lyn was not sure whether to be aghast or astonished, but she managed to blurt out, 'That's not what it looks like.'

Without glancing up she replied, 'That's what it looks like now.'

It was obvious that Lyn was not going to believe her and by now any belief Captain Mirshendy had seemed to have gone. Unfortunately, she was used to people not believing her. She spent the rest of the day in an off centre mood that kept everybody out of her immediate path. Though true to her word she did not wander far, Saranon would save that for later.

She found herself wandering down to where Splodge had just been brought in for the day. He had recovered and was quite placid as she reached out to touch the giant dragon. His trainer Mark who displayed a permanent reminder scarred across his arm, placed there from almost being killed by his favourite pet, had walked off without noticing her. Chelsea one of the handlers, had come in with a big bucket, soap and brushes. Saranon was about to say something, but Chelsea spoke first, 'I don't suppose you want to help?'

Saranon smiled, 'I'd like that.'

As she started to foam up the dragon's filthy coat she began to realise why Chelsea wanted a hand. It was hard physical work which Chelsea made look easy, as she climbed on top of the dragon with a bucket and scrubbed his back. She thought it would be best if she focused on his face first and laughed as she stood back to admire her foamy handy work. Chelsea's voice came from above, 'I wouldn't do that if I were you he doesn't like being laughed at.'

Saranon did her best to put on her serious face and apologised to the dragon.

A deep gruff sound left the dragon's lips, 'That's okay!'

She stared wide eyed up at Chelsea who looked just as shocked and asked, 'Is that normal?'

She had heard that some dragons could speak, but they rarely did so as they considered it to be beneath them. She enjoyed being down in the dragon pens everyone was busy and she could pretend the recent events had not happened. She was convinced that Captain Mirshendy thought the worst of her, even though he had been diplomatic. Saranon looked up from her ponderings and noticed someone trying to get her attention. As she stepped closer she recognised who it was. 'Jedd,' she whispered in amazement.

She felt a wave of relief fall over her as she ducked around the corner. He spoke in a soft voice, 'I haven't got long. Here's your talik and the rest of your belongings.'

He handed her a sova bag, she hesitated a moment then spoke, 'Did you unlock the information?'

'Yes, but I'm afraid I can't help you. My uncle says you've been bonded.'

The look on Saranon's face confirmed it, 'Thank you.'

'I have to go, good luck.'

She watched him disappear into the background. She held the talik close, as if it would somehow wind back time and take her back to Mrs Harper's tavern. For a moment she felt like running away from everything, but it would do no good. She went back and patted the dragon which smelled much cleaner. Chelsea was packing up when Mark came back to check how Splodge was going. He wandered up near Saranon, 'So you're the one causing so much mischief. What will you do with Mitch?'

She looked up startled, he was the mirror image of his dragon, all muscle and worn around the edges.

'I don't have a choice, it is my responsibility to look after him,' she grumbled.

'Yes, but there many kinds of looking after,' Mark exclaimed.

She was not sure where this was leading, but before she could think he had turned to leave and she started to follow. 'I wouldn't do that, when he ends a conversation it's over,' Chelsea spoke.

'What did he mean by that?' She asked.

Chelsea looked at her in disbelief then looked a little closer, 'You don't know do you? Not all bonded wizards are well looked after.'

'I don't understand, but what about the Uvalen Code?' She asked.

'That's only good if you have proof and sometimes that can be difficult. Mark had an aunt, who was mistreated,' Chelsea explained.

'I'm not like that,' she responded.

'You don't need to tell him, if you look after Mitch that will be proof enough,' Chelsea explained.

Saranon shook her head in disbelief and sighed.

Chelsea invited her up to the mess hall it was a grand old room, if she looked above all the marks at table height. They made their way over to where the dragon trainers sat. Unfortunately working with dragons could leave a slight smell behind. For all the wizard's efforts to be rid of it, it still clung in the air. The idea that the smell existed in the first place, meant that anyone who worked with dragons sat with no one else. Chelsea's colleagues now accepted her with hearty grunts of greetings between mouthfuls. The food was better than at the camp, but it was not the same as Mrs Harper's and she started playing with her dinner.

The place was filled with noise. A clanging sound behind her sent a shiver down her spine. She turned around to find several men in a heated argument. There was a brief pause, then one man went hurling into a table and the others for and against took that as their queue to join in. She could not understand what they were saying as they had clouded their voices. She looked at Chelsea who was worried, 'I think we'd better go.'

Chelsea leaned over, and touched Saranon's arm. What was being said came through loud and clear.

'That creature should be restrained.'

'That's none of your business.'

'Oh yes it is and they let her in here.'

She realised they were arguing about her and stood up. She felt an object behind her gliding through the air. She turned and stopped the dagger in the air without moving. There was a moment of pause as the man who held onto the dagger and the others, realised what would have happened. With an all in effort, the man was dragged kicking and screaming out the door. Mark who had not stopped eating through the whole event spoke to Saranon, 'Sit down, you're making a scene.'

Without any further encouragement the atmosphere became a little more tolerable. The group finished the rest of their meal in peace.

She left her strange new friends to check on Mitch who was still in a bad way. Even though he tried to hide it, Rachel was sitting next to him. 'Ah, my two favourite girls,' he remarked.

She felt a bit embarrassed while Mitch made every effort not to look in pain as he reached over and gave her hug. Rachel smiled, 'I'm afraid your new Hilazen is going to have a few more days resting. We heard about what happened in the hall, don't let that trouble you.'

'Thanks,' she responded.

Rachel stood up to go, 'I'll leave you two in peace.'

Mitch waved goodbye, then faced Saranon, 'Are you okay?'

'Yes,' she replied.

'You don't sound so sure,' he commented.

She was going to have to get used to someone knowing her too well. She held his hand in both of hers, 'I feel like I'm going around in circles.'

'Join the club, do you think I like lying in bed doing nothing?' he remarked.

'No. Mitch, are you able to tell me what's going on?' she asked.

'Ah, I was wondering when you were going to ask' he made himself comfortable.

'The Arroada sent a warning with your description. They told us they are the only ones who can look after you. The marks on your hands would prove this.' He leaned closer, 'If you had the marks you would be back in

Darkonia by now. The confusion may have saved you.'

'I thought they were trying to help me. Why would they do this?' she exclaimed.

'Because the Angeon is a powerful being and that scares people,' he answered.

Saranon knew that Mitch was right, but she did not want to admit it, if it were true then Odana had been her saving grace. Her mind started ticking over, 'But that still doesn't explain you.'

'We get on well with the Palascene. Besides, you were doing such a wonderful job cleaning up, that they thought it would be easier if we brought you in,' he spoke.

In the camps she had been one of many in a faceless crowd. Now the thought of being known across several borders was daunting to say the least.

In a short space of time she felt as though she had been thrust to centre stage and no amount of trying to blend into the background would fix it. He lay like a sleeping giant cramped into a bed that was one size too small. He had been honest with her and she felt like she owed him in return. 'Mitch something is wrong with the Keep. It asked for my help and I gave it my word.'

He did not look at her as though she were stupid, in some ways she wished that he did. Instead he gazed at her and spoke in a soft voice, 'Then you have work to do.'

Saranon lay in bed afterwards thinking about what Mitch had said. Her mind was restless and sleep was not going to be of any comfort. She waited a while for the outside noise to settle down. Then she crept down to the indolin chambers and the inner workings of the Keep. In the void of human voices, the soft ramblings of the Keep soaked up through the floor drenching the walls. The sensations made perfect sense to her as she went further down and entered the imbenik chamber closest to her. The Angeon inside intensified with every step as she moved closer to the altar and slid her body down onto the soft surface. She closed her eyes and reached out. Greddin wrapped itself around her in a warm embrace. Her restlessness was swept away replaced by the presence of the Keep.

Saranon was still herself, yet in that moment she was so much more it felt like being home wrapped up in a caring embrace. As she melded with the Keep she could reach further into the mess that had plagued it. In the darkness that surrounded her, she felt parts of herself that had remained dormant rise to the surface. At the same time she felt completely in control and lost in the haze. She opened her eyes and was startled by the sight of the Keep crisscrossing her body. It was gentle yet firm, she raised her arm and the embrace of the Keep moved with her. She rested her arm back down accepting that one of the strangest things came naturally to her.

When the embrace was over she stumbled, forgetting how to walk. For all that had happened it had not disturbed Mitch. Her body was ready for sleep. She made her way back through the corridors with the light from the stars trickling through the windows. 'You don't stay put, do you?' Captain Mirshendy's voice came as he appeared around the corner.

'I send my officers searching for you and you appear out of nowhere.' He grabbed hold of her and held her up against the wall in a cold embrace. Saranon made a small sound in protest.

'Jerald stop that at once! I said stop it,' Rachel had caught up to them, but the Captain would not let go.

The happy dream was over as she realised that Captain Mirshendy was not going to see the situation from her point of view. Before she had a chance to do anything, Rachel had broken the link the Captain was using to keep hold of her. Saranon breathed a sigh of relief as it broke and rubbed her arms.

She had been through enough for one night and if Rachel was going to take on the angry Captain for her, she was not going to complain. She could hear the arguing as they moved further away. She slumped to the floor with exhaustion and the tone of their voices changed. Rachel returned and led her off to bed. Rachel had tears in her eyes. It was hard to know what to say, so she kept her thoughts to herself. As she woke the morning light had been streaming in for some time, but Saranon was trying to ignore it. She was still drained from the night's activities and did not want to face Rachel or the Captain. There was a knock at the door, and Rachel sat down on the bed.

It was an awkward moment, and Saranon spoke first, 'I'm sorry about last night.'

'I know, I was wondering if you could do something for me. Captain Mirshendy needs your help and we both know he's too proud to ask,' Rachel smiled.

The idea of helping the Captain did not exactly appeal to her, but she had not intended to create trouble. If Mitch was right, not helping might do her more harm than good. Rachel continued, 'The Keep has been damaged. Jerald didn't realise you were helping until he sent a crew down to examine what happened. Can forgive him for me?'

Saranon let out one long frustrated sigh, 'I'll see what I can do.'

CHAPTER TWELVE

No easy task

The busy hum of work followed by the occasional sharp clanging noise greeted Saranon as she strode down into the chaos. Covers and lids had been removed. The innards of the Keep were visible everywhere. It was a strange sight to see. Keeps did not like people rummaging around underneath the surface, but this time Greddin Fort was content. It felt like a great sigh of relief stretching into every corner of the building. Captain Mirshendy spotted her and there was a moment of unease as he stared at her with the same cold expression from last night. Regardless of what Rachel had said she would keep out of the Captain's way.

Saranon looked in the other direction and saw two men looking over the makeshift plans she had drawn. It filled her with a sense of pride to be listened to, but it did not seem like a good time to shout with enthusiasm. The wizards around her were already on edge and like so many other things, it could be taken the wrong way. She knew how dangerous the situation was. Captain Mirshendy was keeping a close eye on her while she wandered around. She glanced back and for the first time saw a genuine Palascene, his aura was clear unlike of the others. A wonderful expression of shock creased across the Captain's face as he realised he was standing between the two sorcerers. He side stepped out of the way.

Saranon looked up as though staring into a mirror, and seeing a strange reflection of herself. Then with just as much silence the Palascene left. Normisia had only one sorcerer clan which was then broken down into structured groups and ranks. The Palascene preferred to do things their own way. She went over to Captain Mirshendy looking for answers, but he was not volunteering any. She had been around wizards long enough to know that they had a keen instinct for staying out of sorcerer business.

This infuriated her, as it meant if Saranon was going to introduce herself she would have to do it alone. By the sounds of it they already knew about her. She did not like the idea of forever being a few steps behind. She had a quiet chuckle when she saw Lyn using the drawings she had done earlier to supervise the work. It felt odd to be caught between and the thought made her skin itch. She was still sore from last night and in some ways she hoped that Mitch would be well soon so she could have some sort of privacy. At least the Keep had given up one secret, she now knew what type of sorcerer she was. That coupled with what Jedd had unlocked, left a sour taste in her mouth.

In some ways she was not sure if she should hate herself. Saranon started to think of what people who knew, thought of her, then stopped. If they did, then like the Arroada they could deny her the opportunity to make that choice. Yet the Arroada had let her go in their haste to be rid of her, frightened by what she had done to the Arthrose. Greddin Fort was a stubborn Keep, with an attitude to fight just about anything and if he was your friend he would be that for life. The job was not complete. Just seeing the looks on the wizards' faces, she knew they were cringing at the work fixing the mess would entail. Saranon had one of her bizarre ideas, to her it was normal. After all growing up around people who despised her was normal too.

She managed to track down Rachel who seemed to have a never ending supply of work. She waited a moment before she dropped her great idea into the world. Rachel's stunned silence let her know she was out of touch with reality. 'Do you know how lucky you were, not to be harmed before?' Rachel remarked.

It was the first time Saranon heard how Rachel felt about her joining with the Keep. Rachel took her aside and whispered, 'If you can do that again it will help the Keep, but if something goes wrong we cannot help you.'

She thought she should give it another try and perhaps she would learn more. She waited trying to calm her nerves and took a look around her, for the Keep, it was a matter of time. She had managed to help do the preparation work, but the bulk of it was still to be done and it would take more than one night even if it worked. She found Mitch and as she sat down she felt much older than she was, 'I may be gone for a while.'

'It's not a good time to leave,' he spoke in a firm voice.

'No, I meant I'll still be here just somewhere else,' she added.

'What's going on?' He asked.

'I think the Keep needs me,' she said.

When she saw Mitch again he would be back on his feet, but now was not the time to think about that. This time she knew where to go and what to expect, as the Keep wrapped around her in a warm comforting way. The Keep felt like an extension of her and vice versa. This time she did not need to waste time with introductions, the Keep knew why she was there and if it minded it did not let her know.

Everything seemed so distant, she came with the intention to help and that was what she was going to do. The Keep kept her safe in its warm embrace, protecting her from the outside world. Yet she knew it was not real and it could not last as her senses reached out into the building. Greddin welcomed her as it let her into his thoughts, observing her with a mild curiosity, as she extended her mind through the Keep. She could sense the central core below as it hummed in her mind, calling her from the depths below.

This time she was determined to heal the Keep, even if Greddin showed a small reluctance. As she moved further inward, something was holding her back. Yet that did not deter her as the two worked together to reform the damaged substation. The work was slower than she would have liked and she became annoyed even when the Keep reassured her. For Greddin Fort had a different concept of time and did not share her frustration. He reassured her as they worked and with every step, the Keep retracted his grip on Saranon.

For her it all felt like a deep sleep, only her mind remained active. When she woke it took her a while to realise how much time had passed. She had lost three weeks, Greddin Fort was back to normal, but she was not sure about herself. She hesitated before standing up, waiting for her legs to work again. Her muscles were sore, even though she had been lying down the whole time. Saranon had used a great deal of energy and the exhaustion hit as she stumbled before reaching the door. She placed her hand against the wall to steady herself as she caught her breath. Saranon hoped that what she had done would be enough.

Saranon opened the seal on the door and stepped out of the chamber. Mitch was waiting for her on the other side, she should have guessed. She had forgotten how tall he was, Mitch hesitated before helping her up to the habitable area of the Keep. She tried to say something, but he did not notice Saranon knew he was ignoring her. It was night time above ground and Mitch with all the care in the world helped her get ready for bed. She noticed her quarters had changed from amongst the wizards, to an area set aside for guests. The place was more welcoming and larger. Not that she minded the cramped little room, but bigger just seemed so much better.

He was being too nice, she was starting to suspect that something was going on, 'Mitch.'

She gave him such a strange look that he knelt down beside the bed, 'Did you forget about the ceremony?'

'I didn't spend much time reading,' she responded.

'Well, it's like this, I have to be nice for the ceremony,' he smiled.

'I think I preferred your old self,' she exclaimed.

'You know I can't be that,' he replied.

Saranon wondered what the others thought of her melding with the Keep, 'I hope I didn't get you into trouble, being away for so long.'

'No, but you gave the Palascene something to talk about,' he said.

Saranon curled up on the floor watching the dying embers in the fireplace. He sat down beside her, and placed his arm around her, 'I'm not going to get any sleep tonight am I?'

Mitch comforted her as the embers went out. She hated to admit it, but part of her needed him to be there.

She could manage, but Mitch seemed to make things easier. She wondered if it was like that with other bonds. He stayed and comforted her without question. The next day started with a loud clattering noise followed by raised voices. Her eyes opened into the bright sunlight streaming in from the early morning. She had almost forgotten what sunlight was like. It felt like a dream until Saranon dashed over to open the window, and the warmth came streaming through. As the Keep had instructed, she dressed in robes more appropriate for her kind. They were casual, yet still held an elegant sombre look, meant for one much older than she.

As she was fixing the finishing touches the door burst open and Chelsea burst through. It took her a while to remember who Chelsea was. There was a moment of awkward silence as the two girls stared at each other. 'People are wondering what you will do with Mitch. Sometimes bad things happen to wizards that get bonded,' Chelsea spoke in haste.

'I would like to say I can keep him safe, but I'm not sure,' she replied.

'Just say you don't intend to hurt him,' Chelsea asked.

'At the moment he is the last person I would want to...' she began.

'Good, now come with me,' her friend spoke in haste.

They tried to scamper past a few Palascene, she was held up with courteous greetings. Chelsea had moved on ahead before noticing that Saranon was holding a conversation. As she joined up with her friend, Chelsea yanked her arm, 'Do you know what you just did?'

'I was being polite,' she suggested.

Chelsea gave a look of exasperation, 'I meant that was too good, flawless.'

Saranon still did not understand. 'Be careful, you don't want to give people the wrong impression,' Chelsea added.

'In case you hadn't noticed, the Palascene have been

judging me ever since I arrived,' she replied.

'I just hope you know what you're doing,' Chelsea responded.

While the two girls were talking they managed to walk right past Mark who had been looking for them 'Hey!'

The girls turned at once and Mark continued, 'Do you know where I can find the owner of a large male marmoz dragon with a scar on his hind leg?'

Saranon felt the blood draining away from her face, 'I thought he had gone back to Alveron.'

'Right,' Mark nudged the girls forward until they were downstairs in the dragon pens.

The dragon that she had ridden all the way from Alveron was curled up in ball resting in one of the pens. 'I take it he didn't return home?' She remarked.

'Thanks to you, he doesn't have a home. Katholomu's previous owners do not want him back,' Mark spoke.

She reached out and touched the beautiful creature. Mark continued, 'I wouldn't send him back anyway, he hasn't been looked after.'

'Did you buy him?' Chelsea asked, 'You did.'

Saranon was wondering what on earth she would do with a docile giant that could kill at a moment's notice. Not the sort of thing one left lying around the home for guests to walk into. Nonetheless she did feel sorry for it, like her, the dragon had travelled far from home. 'I can look after him while you're here, but you'll need to spend time with him,' Mark spoke.

She could not help it, she felt a little tear drop escape

down her cheek.   She wished there had been someone like Mark to come along and rescue her from the camp before Tasha had died. The dragon was as soft as she remembered, with muscles as hard as stone.

The marmoz were not the most favoured among wizard clans, due to their stubborn nature. Yet, at the same time, they were well respected for being fierce fighters. Saranon was unsure of what to say, no one had given her a dragon before. In fact no one had given her much at all. She was used to finding her own way. The dragon moved its head and she looked behind her to see Mitch talking with Mark.

She whispered to Chelsea, 'I'm doomed aren't I?'

Chelsea gave her a puzzled look. 'The ceremony,' Saranon said.

'Oh it's not that bad, well, if your idea of bad consists of a bunch old people droning on, then yeah.'

'That's not funny,' she remarked.

Mark's voice boomed, 'Hey, he's not a toy. I didn't say clamber all over him.'

Saranon and Chelsea stepped away from the dragon with innocent expressions across their faces. She was about to say something to Mitch, but thought better of it. Instead the two girls started running off in the opposite direction.

Chelsea had work to do, so Saranon kept her own company. Mitch had left her with some reading material. He had given this to her before she had linked with the Keep and now it was looking rather tattered around the edges. The dragon pens were not the cleanest of place, but they were kept tidy. An improvement to what she had grown up with. Saranon made herself at home. For all her good intentions, trying to understand the way wizards did things, was rather difficult. A few times she looked up at Chelsea wondering if she should ask, her frustration showing on her face.

The more she became frustrated the more Chelsea found the whole situation funny, 'Why don't you ask Rachel?'

'I wouldn't want to bother her,' she replied.

'Well don't look at me, I'm not going to help,' Chelsea grinned.

Saranon sat in a grump, tolerating her friend's amusement. She could not see the funny side at all. She finally gave in and wandered upstairs, there was a neat little staircase tucked away in the middle of a great arch. She turned to look at Chelsea, 'I'm going.'

'Of course you are,' Chelsea grinned while holding a dirty rag in one hand.

The staircase was narrow and was only large enough for one. She half ran to the top, almost pelting head first into a Palascene. Bianca did not seem to notice Saranon's folly, 'Were you trying to impress us by winning the Keep's trust?'

Saranon hesitated for moment before answering, 'I did not win anything.'

'That is not what I heard about your wizard,' the Palascene responded.

Saranon knew she was referring to Mitch, 'That was

different.'

'So you fall for the first man that comes along, whatever he is,' Bianca did not see any need to accept Saranon as one of her own. She walked away with a self-absorbed air of confidence.

Saranon could tell that had been no idle chat. The Palascene had been keeping their distance watching and waiting for signs of trouble. It drove her mad thinking about it, but there was nothing she could do. She was caught in a slow moving game and if she moved too fast, it could all come undone. Not that she was used to seeing things unravel, but this time it would be nice to succeed, and do things right. She did not have a clue about the inner workings of wizardry and it would be embarrassing to mess up at the ceremony. To her surprise Rachel for once had a lack of things to do and was taking her time tidying up the place.

'Rachel,' she asked.

'Yes Saranon,' Rachel replied.

'I was wondering if you could help me, you see I'm a bit stuck with these,' she pulled out the tattered bits of paper.

'Well for starters you will need this one,' Rachel pulled out a small booklet.

Rachel placed it on the table where they both sat. While Saranon was still frustrated she asked questions. Somehow it did not seem like a completely foreign language when Rachel explained it, which was a relief. For a while she was thinking she would have no hope of understanding and would end up making a fool of herself. It was difficult imagining having to put up with Mitch for the rest of her life.

There were some ways of breaking a bond, but from what she understood trying to undo the situation would only make things worse. For some reason wizards hated the thought of having a bond broken more than being stuck with one. It was an interesting concept which had helped give Saranon a bit of leeway. The bond had been tough for people like Captain Mirshendy to get used to. The thought of the Captain popped into her head as she realised he had joined them out on the deck overlooking the gardens. He came up and placed his hand on her shoulder, 'Now you are going to behave for the ceremony.'

'Jerald you are interrupting,' Rachel spoke.

The Captain looked down at the table, 'Oh.' For a second the Captain was lost for words, 'Carry on.'

Rachel was unimpressed by the Captain's attempt at backing out of an awkward moment. Saranon saw a glance she recognised, 'You two are going to be married.'

'What?' The lovers spoke at once.

The Captain realised he had given something away and went, leaving Rachel caught in the middle. Saranon continued on oblivious, 'You would make a nice pair, at least the Keep thinks so.'

The Captain who had not travelled far, ducked his head back around the corner. 'You can't say something like that,' he spoke.

'Why not?' She remarked.

'To begin with Rachel and I are not getting married,' the Captain added.

Rachel was aghast, 'Why not?'

The Captain realised what he had just said in front of his girlfriend, 'You know what I meant.'

'No, I didn't,' Rachael exclaimed.

'I just meant I think you both would make a nice couple,' Saranon knew as soon as the words came out that they sounded pathetic.

'It's all right Saranon just continue reading, the Captain and I need to talk,' Rachel stood up and left.

She was thinking herself lucky. She had avoided the complications of having a boyfriend on top of everything else.

CHAPTER THIRTEEN

The Host

It was a sleepless night that racked at Saranon's mind and kept her stirring well into the early hours. The past few days had flown by so fast that she had no time to catch a moment to herself. Between Rachel who had taken time off work, Chelsea, and Katholomu her time was all but taken up. She had been quite happy to let the time slip away. After all she had sacrificed three weeks to the Keep and what were a few extra days in comparison. Still for someone who was supposed to be in charge of her own life she was finding it difficult to stay focused on her agenda. She felt a tingle run through her arms and looked up to see Greddin moving a little in a strange manner. The faint flows of energy that she could see running through the ceiling had changed.

Her senses told her that it was not a good sign, but

she was still half asleep. It did not take long to prepare herself, as she went to pick up Tellembre she felt the Keep shudder. Now that was a bad sign, Saranon went to open the door, but someone on the other side did first. It was an elderly wizard, she could make out William Trazen in the first rays of day light and realised he had come to begin the ceremony. She was about to say something about Greddin Fort. Yet the look on the grand old wizard's face made her have second thoughts. The Cryzinelan wizards were strange. They were comfortable being open without giving anything important away. For all their friendliness towards her, she had been able to get much less out of them than their Alveronian counterparts.

They prided themselves on their differences. This could be quite frustrating as Saranon had found out on a few occasions. Chelsea had been a good friend, but for all her youth she let little slip. She felt awkward being chaperoned. William's arm felt like solid steel, as he held it firm for her to hold onto while he lead the way. She had asked Greddin about the ceremony, but unfortunately Keeps had a different take on human activities. Inside she wanted to let out a cry, staying calm and quiet was not her strong point. The urge to break the silence was tingling up her spine like a bad itch. The Keep had settled down, perhaps she had been overreacting and everything would be fine.

Of course it was not fine, her mind was starting to ramble through a hundred different thoughts cramming for attention. Saranon was trying not to sweat. Yet the last time the Cryzinelan had taken the initiative they had thought that abducting her was good idea. She wondered if the wizards would be more open after the ceremony. Then she sensed a familiar voice from the depths, it is time. Greddin was a wizards' Keep much to the annoyance of the Palascene, who had great difficulty using the areas within. William was leading her into a part of the Keep which was known as a wizards' only domain.

For Saranon it was like travelling, underwater not that breathing in water was a problem for a sorceress, but it just felt wrong. She took a deep breath and entered the large passage mindful that being here was not the safest place. The Keep had been matter of fact, when it stated that it was much easier for wizards in a stronghold to kill sorcerers. A lone one would not be much trouble. Keeps could live for hundreds of years and were used to humans having short life spans in comparison. Greddin would look out for her to a certain extent because of what she was. Still that did not help the uneasy feeling weighing her down.

It was hard not to let out a faint laugh at the serious faces, but she managed to control herself. The wizards greeted her as if for the first time, then William led her into a small chamber. As Chelsea had warned her, the ceremony involved a lot of reciting which William managed in a monotone voice. In any other situation it would have been enough to make her fall asleep. She was proud of managing to recite her own parts in a serious voice and hoped they could not tell what she was thinking on the inside. Mitch was not present for this part so she felt quite alone. She focused on William's voice. '…And do you accept the responsibility of guiding Mitchell Kregner in the ways of the Cryzinelan…'

Saranon was able to get through the first part without falling asleep. The second part involved dunking poor Mitch underwater to symbolise the start of a new beginning. Unfortunately she was rather small and meek in comparison. So it turned into a spectacle when she lost her grip on the smooth surface and got a dunking as well. She was upset about messing the whole thing up. She resurfaced to find William, Mitch and several onlookers roaring with laughter. The dunking had taken the serious edge off the rest of the ceremony and it had helped ease the tension much to Saranon's relief. Being drenched in the sacred waters of the inner stronghold was not an experience she wanted to be reminded about. Though in the Keep news travelled fast.

She had dried the water off, but when Chelsea visited her she may as well have been soaking wet. 'I can't believe you fell in,' Chelsea said with a cheesy grin.

'Well it wasn't what I was aiming to do,' she exclaimed.

Mitch was minding his own business sorting out a few gifts he had been given while the two girls chatted away. If the ceremony was anything to go by with Saranon it was going to be different, perhaps in a good way. He could think of a few sorcerers that would have had a bad reaction to being laughed at, but she had taken it quite well. He had been given some nice clothes and other items, all rather useful.

He stayed with her during the night curled up on the floor near the fireplace on a cosy makeshift bed. Saranon could not sleep she should have been able to after the day's events, but something was not right. After having been connected to the Keep for so long, she could feel its daily patterns were a little out of sync. As she stared up at the ceiling the energy fluctuated again. 'Did you notice anything?' She asked Mitch.

'No,' he replied.

She was not convinced that it had been her imagination and decided it would need investigating later.

She had become sick of staying within the confines of the Keep. She was longing to get out to enjoy the beautiful sunny morning and see her old friends who had welcomed her into their midst. 'Mitch, I don't mean to be rude, but I would like to leave Greddin and visit my friends.'

'That's fine William just wanted you stay in the town of Redadere,' he remarked.

Saranon almost fumed, 'You mean I could have done that any time!'

Mitch realised what he said and tried to back track, 'Well I don't think…'

'I'm getting some fresh air. Now did you want to join me?' She asked.

'It's best if I do just for the moment,' he added.

'Good, now are there any more surprises that I need to know,' she asked.

Mitch grinned, 'No.'

'Are you sure?' She snapped.

'I think it's time you got out for a while,' he suggested.

The two left the Keep and went out into the busy streets of the second largest city in Normisia. It did not take long to find Celia, or more to the point her friend found Saranon. Mitch blended into the background while the two acted like boisterous teenagers. Saranon found out that the wiccan had been worried about her, and with good reason. Celia was having trouble not knowing whether to laugh or cry as she explained what had happened. It appeared that the Palascene wanting to palm off the hard work to the wizards had backfired. At this pointed she noticed Mitch was trying not show he was listening, but she could tell he was interested.

Her wiccan friends loved gossip. Celia was in her element as she told Saranon the Palascene had not expected her to be so tolerant of wizards. This had led them to the dilemma of having to accept her in some form. This had disgruntled the Arroada who had sent them after her in the first place. This was all starting to sound too confusing. Yet she understood the part where the Palascene did not like being told what to do by the Arroada. She listened to how the whole arrangement had fallen apart. Of course this took the most part of the morning and the afternoon to explain, back in the privacy of Mrs Harper's Tavern. Saranon was surprised to find that Mitch did not seem out of place. He greeted Mrs Harper with a warm embrace as though they were long lost friends.

Celia noticed her puzzled look. 'We usually get along well with our neighbours, even if they have different ways of doing things.'

'You're not wrong there. I feel like the more I find out the less I understand,' she commented.

'Well you'll have to learn pretty quick seeing as Mitch will likely follow you anywhere. I never did find out about how you ended up with him?' Celia quizzed.

Saranon cringed while thinking about it, 'It's complicated.'

'That's all right. We've had more trouble since you left, more wiccan have gone missing. Jedd thinks they won't be coming back, it's pretty serious,' Celia spoke in a soft tone.

'If you want, I can stay longer?' She asked.

'I was hoping you would,' Celia added.

Mitch was fine with staying late and Saranon was looking forward to being able to relax if only for a moment.

When Jedd came in from a hard day's work she had trouble recognising him, the stress had made him look older. Celia left while the two spoke, it did not take long for her to figure out that the fluctuations within the Keep, may be related. It seemed that while she had been busy repairing the Keep, someone else had been busy trying to attack it. Taking control of a Keep was a lucrative prospect for those who travelled the tainted path. Yet a Keep, the size of Greddin, was usually safe. The sheer size alone and power behind it deterred all but the craziest. Perhaps they were going after a smaller Keep, but as Jedd said, they had seen no signs of anyone going after some of the smaller ones.

Saranon tried to enjoy the rest of the evening. Her

friends had no trouble doing so. It was getting smoky in the air so she went outside with Mitch following not far behind. He spoke first, 'So what do you think?'

'Well, I'm not sure to be honest it could just be…'

She was distracted by a fast moving cart coming their way. It looked familiar, 'Is that what I think it is?'

Mitch turned and waved as the Captain stepped down prompting them to climb on. She hesitated out of exasperation before squeezing between the Captain and Mitch. 'You owe me an explanation,' she glared at him.

The Captain was none too keen about having her that close but proceeded anyway. 'We're having trouble back at Greddin.'

'Mrs Harper said wiccan were going missing, and it had escalated in the last few days' Mitch spoke.

Saranon's brain worked overtime as Mitch, and the Captain spoke around her. She was trying to think back to her discussions with the Keep.

She was about to say something as Mitch turned toward her and whispered, 'We have to go.'

She gave him a disapproving look as the wheels of the cart rolled underneath. She took a last glimpse of Mrs Harper's Tavern before letting out a heavy sigh. She could feel a sense of urgency well up in him, as she tried to read his thoughts that remained forever clouded. For the third time she found herself in the cart moving toward Greddin Fort, although this time had she climbed in by herself.

She sighed in a mix of frustration as the great doors leading into the Keep closed behind her. The thought to scream and shout like last time was tempting and Mitch gave her a stern look as though reading her mind. Saranon could sense the energy of the Keep as it shimmered along the wall in an uneven pattern. The image made a shiver run down her spine, as she followed the Captain down below the habitable area. The air was dry as it hummed along with a faint breeze from the vents rising through the building. She stayed out of the way behind Mitch, as they approached a small gathering that appeared ready for anything. She wondered what she had just walked into.

Deep in the bowels of the Keep, Captain Mirshendy lead the team to check out some strange disturbances that had created a dead zone. No one felt comfortable when part of the Keep was down. For all the repairs that had been done, it had not gone anywhere near to fixing all the problems that sprang up. The Captain's troops were more than capable, but it was dangerous work. They stayed close together, this was no time to get lost. As they travelled closer to the area, the Captain realised that it had been flooded. It was not the worst problem, wizards were good at adapting, but flooding an area often hid other dangers. 'Can you send a sensor down to check it out?' The Captain asked his officer.

'Way ahead of you,' Nathan spoke.

The little beacon shot off into the dark water. Nathan waited near the edge, 'It's not sending back anything we're going to have to try somewhere else.'

'All right pack up and we'll move around to the east. There's an opening we can try there.'

Nathan turned away from the water to join the others. Just as he did something dark sprang out of the water grabbing his leg and yanking him down. One of his colleagues tried to get hold of his arm, but he was being dragged in as well. The Captain yelled for the second man to let go amid the turmoil. The last thing they saw was Nathan's petrified look as he went under without a trace. 'We're getting out of here now,' the Captain yelled.

There was no need to explain why as they ran back into the secure part of the Keep. Saranon could sense an odd energy rise from the depths and she needed no convincing to leave as she ran with the small group. The Captain walked straight into the control room where Lyn was running around in a mad panic. The information filled the screen as it was relaying back from the Keep. 'I just lost one of my men,' the Captain spoke.

'I know,' Lyn replied.

'Can you at least tell me what that was?' He asked with a sense of urgency.

'I'm trying as fast as I can,' she spoke.

The Captain stepped aside, 'I thought you knew what we were going into.'

'There's no way of telling in a dead zone, I just need some time to find out,' Lyn exclaimed.

'You had better have an answer,' with that the Captain walked away.

As the first light ran in through the open windows near where the Captain had been waiting all night, Lyn rushed in, her face paler than usual. 'I'm sorry I think

Nathan is being made into a Host.'

'How long do we have?' He asked.

'We've already lost four hours,' Lyn replied.

'So fifty-six hours remaining,' the Captain was not impressed.

He thumped his fist hard down on the table, how could he have been so stupid. Whoever was trying to take over the Keep had what they wanted. It would not be long before it would become impossible to stop.

Saranon caught the last few words, 'What do you mean?'

'I lost one of my men and now he's being turned into a Host for the Keep,' the Captain said in a flat tone before looking away.

This was all new territory for her. She was beginning to feel as though everything was fast spiralling out of control. Her stomach hit rock bottom as her mind raced, it was all happening too fast and she felt like she was being left behind. She left the control room, she would get no answers there, especially since it was so crowded. She would have to find another way to access the information she needed.

An awful pained sound came from behind, Saranon returned to see the Captain curled up on the ground, 'What's going on?'

Mitch whispered, 'Rachel has been taken.'

'We are in deep trouble, aren't we?' She exclaimed.

'You could say that,' Mitch replied.

It did not take long for the Captain to regain his

composure. This time, whatever was going on, it had become personal.

She wanted to reach out and help, but everywhere she looked the situation seemed to be have slipped beyond her. Captain Mirshendy saw her look and gave her a comforting pat on the shoulder, 'We'll get Rachel back.'

Saranon was not so sure. The Captain was preparing a small group to go out into the dead zone and she caught Mitch in the middle of getting ready. She gave him a disapproving look, but there was no point trying to stop him. If Rachel was in trouble he would follow the Captain anywhere.

She started getting ready to go with them, Mitch looked surprised and disgruntled, 'You are not coming with us.'

'It's all right' the Captain replied.

Mitch glared at her for intruding on his work then handed her a weapon. Saranon looked at it puzzled, 'What do I need that for?'

'For protection,' he explained.

She handed it back, 'I'm not going to need it.'

'Suit yourself,' he remarked.

Mitch was not going to get into an argument with her. If she wanted to go out into the dead zone unprepared, he was not going to bail her out. Saranon could not think of anything else to do and perhaps getting a closer look at the situation would help. From what she heard, it would be difficult to make it any worse. So, armed with that knowledge she stayed close to Mitch and travelled down into unchartered territory. She was used to hiding and a few times when the group had stopped she had blended into the wall. The first time it scared one of the soldiers standing next to her, but they had bigger things to worry about. The Keep was still operational, even though it was not much use as it could not be relied on.

This was the second time she had entered into a dead zone, the area where the Keep had lost control. Odana back in Alveron had remained calm. He had experienced many small glitches before and that was how he viewed them. Greddin was having great difficulty and had gone into a panic, which was not helping Saranon at all. Strange noises started muffling their way along to where they were and she listened. Unlike the mess in the control room some of it was making sense, 'Get back!'

She did not need to push Mitch out of the way, as the wizards cleared out of sight. The whooshing sound was now audible over the background noise. She had an intense urge to go out of her hiding place and deal with it, but she could not. Instead she held back a yell as a cold hard icy flame of sorcery whirled past them at phenomenal speed. The sound as it passed through, was deafening, she let out a yell that disappeared in the noise as she held on. Then it was gone.

Saranon crumbled in the silence that followed, Mitch bent down and picked her up. They had no time to waste and in true wizard fashion the best time to strike was after a great deal of energy had been expended by the enemy. She pulled at his arm and whispered, 'No.'

It was too late, whether she wanted to or not she felt like she was being pulled into the heart of a wasps nest. As the wizards attacked back, another ball of ice flew past only just missing the Captain, but that did not deter any of them. Instead the wizards went to action closing in as they struck back and the air soon filled with the hollow smell of wizardry. The smell burnt as it hit her lungs and made her gag. As much as she liked being on the same side as the wizards, it was beginning to have a few draw backs.

Saranon stopped to catch her breath and Mitch called out, 'Next time you should stay at home.'

'This is your home,' she said between coughing. 'And I'm not going.'

She ran after them not wanting to be left behind. The haze was thick, she could see two had been injured. She admired their strength, they were relentless. She wondered how she would have fared on the receiving end, then thought better of it. The Captain had sent for backup and she could make out a few new faces that had caught up with them. As she turned around, it took her a while to realise the only sound anyone was making was her coughing.

Saranon went closer to see what was going on. She could see several sorcerers and they had the one person that would make Captain Mirshendy stop. Rachel was kneeling on a small stone floor that stood out above a murky liquid. She recognised the liquid, sheal it could absorb almost anything including sorcery. Rachel was in the middle on a small island, just big enough to hold her. The wizards had rushed in and for the time being were an excellent cover.

They had managed a stalemate. While blocking the sorcery it created a beautiful deadly light works that crinkled across the air. Rachel looked over and saw her. Saranon knew she had to do something, the sheal was rising it was painful to watch.

Once it reached Rachel, her energy would be absorbed and flow into the Keep. At that moment one of the sorcerers managed to break through and two wizards disintegrated from sight. The sorcery hit Saranon with a wave of heat it filled her lungs and made her feel alive. She looked down at her arm and realised her body was consuming the energy. She looked up at the sorcerers and saw their faces as they realised they were in serious trouble. The three scrambled for the door, Mitch tried to latch onto the last one, but he managed to get away. Through all the excitement she rescued Rachel, and could only just hear her shouting.

Rachel grabbed her hand and shoved it in the sheal for a second. All the energy that she had absorbed drained with it. 'Ah! What did you do that for,' Saranon cried holding her hand.

'You absorbed too much energy,' Rachel responded.

Her hand throbbed, 'It's nice to see you too. Do have you any idea how much that hurts?'

'You wanted to come,' Mitch reminded her.

Rachel fell in behind where it was safe, while she clutched her hand in a grump. The wizards moved on, Nathan was still out there and time was running short.

CHAPTER FOURTEEN

Taking on the Dihan

Saranon's pulse was racing fast with both fear and excitement. The wizards around her were travelling fast and she was finding it hard to keep up. A glimmer of movement caught her eye and she realised the sorcerers were behind her. As she panicked she tripped over, the sorcerers muffled the sound so as not to alert the wizards and she was on her own. She could see Addison striding towards her. She could see a few sealed doorways and tried to go through one, but it would not budge. She kept on running, she sensed the sorcerer behind her preparing to attack. With all her might she managed to push herself through one of the seals. The blast of sorcery from behind just missed her hand as she plunged through.

Saranon turned and trembled as she tried to scream at what she saw, but nothing came out. She saw what had been done to Nathan, the seal was glowing and she realised Addision was trying to get through. Before she could protect the seal it had already closed and she was locked inside with the Host. She scrambled across the room to try and find another way out. 'I thought you would be pleased to see me again,' the Keep spoke.

The words came out of Nathan's mouth, but they were not his. She forced herself to look at what had been done, 'You look terrible.'

As Saranon listened to herself she wanted to take the words back. The Host laughed, it was not yet complete but it was aware of its surroundings. She forced herself to sit down beside it. She watched as the Keep melded part of itself to what was once Nathan. Once the process was complete Nathan would be part of the Keep and vice versa. He tried to hold out his hand and she held it. It felt strange and she almost dry reached. The Host seemed oblivious to her difficulties and relaxed. 'You look different,' Saranon spoke.

Nathan still looked human, he stared up with his jet black eyes giving away what he was and would become, 'I should hope so.'

Saranon felt a tear travel down the side of her cheek. There were a couple of loud blasts from the outside, 'What will you do?' She asked.

'You don't like my decision?' The Keep asked.

'No, I meant about them,' she spoke as she stared at where the opening had been.

'You disapprove, would you rather I give myself to the

Palascene?'

'To be honest I think neither is worthy,' she exclaimed.

Nathan laughed, 'Perhaps you're right.'

Saranon did not want to look away for fear of offending the Keep so the two remained silent as the process continued. In the corridor Addison was fuming as he realised she was with the Host. He hurled his sorcery full pelt at the locked seal, but only managed to knock himself back with the blast. The noise brought the wizards running back and he blocked their blows as he ran with the others. The wizards fell back leaving Saranon behind, she could sense Mitch moving further away and wanted to shout out but it would be no use.

The wall was stone cold and there was no way out, she had been locked in with the Host. She slid down onto the floor in a sign of resignation, it was all she could think of as Nathan lay in front of her. The process was slow she knew that all she could do was wait. There was no point trying to help Nathan, he was already part of the Keep. Trying to stop what was happening would kill him, and anger Greddin Fort. It took a great amount of energy to create a Host and the Keep did not always accept the offering. Either way, she wondered if whoever made him knew what they were doing. A short term gain came with all sorts of risks. Nathan would not be as easy to subdue as the Keep.

Hosts had a reputation for being uncontrollable and the description reminded her of herself. Saranon stood up and sat on the raised stone table staring down at Nathan, it was like waiting for the inevitable. Nathan was awake and spoke to her in a soft voice. Now that she had overcome the shock it did not seem so bad, but still she was having trouble seeing the dangerous side of it all. Perhaps it was just misunderstood like she was. She had had enough of being labelled by other people.

The Keep made a strange noise and she looked over her shoulder. Nathan grabbed her and shoved her onto the floor, the process was finished. Saranon tried to push him off, but he was much stronger, she shouted at him to no affect. He stared at her, then leaned down and kissed her, then brushed his fingers through her hair.

He whispered, 'Don't you want to play?'

'You and I have more important things to do. Now get off!' She shouted.

The Host hesitated for a while smiled and helped her up. Nathan took a few steps then turned and laughed, 'Did you think I would let you go?'

'You don't own me,' she said.

'I don't need to,' he replied.

'I helped you,' she snapped.

'Yes, you did. Tell you what we'll do…you don't like being kissed do you,' he smiled.

'Next time ask,' she glared at him.

'Someone's a little touchy, are you like that with Mitch?' He asked.

'No,' she replied in a harsh tone.

The Host took Saranon's bond-breaker Corsavere off her and she yelled, 'Give it back!'

He held it out of reach, 'Did you want it?'

'Nathan, give me the bond-breaker!' She yelled.

'No, I think I'll keep it,' he taunted.

'Nathan!' She shouted.

A shuddering noise echoed through the locked seal, someone was trying to get in. Saranon turned to the Host, 'Is there another way out?'

'Of course,' he replied.

The two made their way out through a narrow passage. While Nathan taunted her by holding the bond-breaker just out of reach. Behind them came a crashing sound as the seal broke and they ran even faster. The two scrambled into a large chamber, she stayed close to Nathan and he smiled, 'I thought you didn't like me.'

She did not answer, the sorcerers were catching up fast. The Host looked at her, 'So what's the plan?'

'I thought you had one,' she replied.

'You place great faith in me,' the Host retorted.

Saranon knew what he meant, the Keep was not designed to deal with this type of conflict and she felt alone. At least Nathan had led them into one of the main chambers where the Keep was stronger. Yet the connection was still down, and the place felt cold. She asked, 'Can you…'

Nathan was one step ahead, he had gone to one of the corners to try and bring the Keep back online. She felt her panic rising, she had no idea what to do and she felt small in the centre of the room. The sorcerers had taken the long way which was easier to travel. Though it would not be long and they would be through the door, Saranon tried to stay calm.

In the middle of the dead zone it did not take much before the giant doors gave way. At first there was nothing, then she heard the sound of their hollow laughing. The sorcerers were already in the room, she could see them. She looked up to where Nathan had been and there was no trace of him. She knew that no one was close, but losing sight of Nathan was not good. She ran to find him and hit a barrier of energy. She realised she was trapped, this was beginning to be a common occurrence. She had to get out, she placed her hands up against the barrier something was wrong.

It felt strange and she thought against trying to go through it. That would have been the straight forward option, but not doing so meant she was still trapped. There was definitely no sign of Nathan, as Saranon realised that the sorcerers had dealt with her. She sensed the other wizards approaching, Mitch ran up to the barrier and was about to do something. Saranon waved her arms to stop him, and he pulled up just in time, 'What is it?'

'There something different about the barrier, they've got Nathan,' she replied.

Captain Mirshendy spoke up, 'You saw Nathan?'

'You're trapped,' Mitch smiled.

Saranon turned to Mitch, 'It's not funny.' She turned to the Captain, 'Yes he was fine, but he ran off with my bond-breaker.'

Mitch found the whole situation amusing, 'Do you want some help?'

Saranon glared at him as he removed the barrier, she was not impressed about being shown up by a wizard.

The Captain thought out loud, 'So now we've lost a Host and your bond-breaker.'

'Yes,' Saranon said.

She realised that she had made a mess of the situation and Mitch was not showing her any support. She kept pace with the wizards as they searched for Nathan and saw that Bianca had joined them. She paid no attention to Saranon, but then she had expected that. They met up with a small group of Palascene and the problem became clear. Her heart sank with despair she wanted to help, but everything she seemed to touch was going wrong.

The Dihan who had been trying to take over the Keep, were so close to success. The desperation showed on the otherwise calm Palascene. She wanted to apologise, but there would be no apology great enough to make up for this. The Dihan had sealed off the area where they were holding Nathan and she waited as the group tried to find a way in. Bianca found a small weakness in the barrier, it was enough for them to go through. Saranon wanted to go with the sorcerers, but it was made clear that she had to stay behind. The Captain and Mitch were not impressed, there was no way they could make it through without trying to break the barrier.

She kicked her heel against the wall, patience was not her strong point, the Captain made it appear easy. A few strange sounds could be heard through the small opening, then a harrowing loud scream followed by stone cold silence. The Captain looked at Saranon, 'Perhaps you had better take a look?'

'I'm not going in there,' she exclaimed.

Mitch picked her up and shoved her through the barrier with her kicking. 'That could've hurt,' she said.

'Don't make me come after you,' he spoke.

She tried to get back on the other side, but Mitch stood in her way, 'I think you owe us a favour.'

Saranon knew that he was right. Although it did not make it any less scary as she made her way through the opening that led down a small creepy tunnel. The thought occurred to her that the Dihan would be expecting someone else to come, she hated surprises. The tunnel was deadly silent and she made slow progress. It occurred to her that Mitch may have been able to go through the barrier, but she was too far along now. The tunnel opened up to several different paths, she went left. Passing through another barrier before she knew what she had done.

The barrier remained silent she took a deep breath and moved on. She could hear people and did not know who they were. One of the Dihan was standing up ahead, there would be no way she could get closer without making a scene. She was caught between doing nothing and moving forward. If she went back now, Mitch would not be impressed. The possibility of something going wrong scared her, but then she had already done that. Her skin went cold. She had to remain in her current form, even though it would leave her blind to many things.

Saranon doubted whether anything she did would

make a difference, she would just have to try and hope. It was difficult to see, then with so much sorcery hanging thick in the air it was hard to make out anything. The sorcerer in front of her fell silent on the floor when she removed her bond-breaker. The movement was quick and fluid with a muffled sound. She found her way through the haze and what she saw did not look good. The place was filled with a strange light, which filtered through from the heart of the Keep in an open conduit covering most of the floor.

The Dihan had more than just the Host, the Palascene had been captured. She made it down to the conduit, Addison was lying in wait. 'Ah, so nice of you to join the party. Thanks for the gift.'

He held Saranon's bond-breaker Corsavere, 'Now the question is what I should do with you?'

Addison leaped back, floating above the conduit, she tried to get closer, but the energy was too intense. The sorcerer lashed out and she ran to find cover. The flare of sorcery prickled as it frayed along the edges of the blast. Saranon could see Bianca's frightened stare from the corner of the room where she was being held.

Saranon took a deep breath she had to concentrate and the energy running from the conduit was not helping. She tried to become the Angeon something was holding her back, she tried again and it only made her feel sick. She would have to find some other way to fight and then she remembered Nathan had kissed her. She could try to take control of the Host, but would it work? There was only one way to find out. There was a small conduit running up through the wall close by, she ran over and pulled the seal open. It was going to take all her strength and she was pelted backward with the blow. It had not worked, but that was no deterrent. Saranon was not used to giving up. She looked back, Addison was getting ready to fire again, she gave as much as she could, there was something blocking her.

She tried even harder as the blast roared over her head she ducked and stared down at the conduit in dismay, at least she had tried. Addison's screams cut through the air and she ran back to find that Nathan had broken free. Addison turned towards Saranon, 'This is your fault!'

He lunged towards her and Saranon could feel the Angeon rise though it did not strike out. Corsavere started burning out of control in Addison's hand and he had to let go. The Dihan joined their leader, and ran towards the Angeon. Their sorcery held the full blast of their fury as it hit her. Sparking with great intensity and causing confusion.

She could hear Bianca crying out to her as the Angeon disintegrated her opponents into ash. The conduit that Addison had opened, was still flooding energy through the Keep she walked toward the massive hole. Bianca yelled behind her, 'No!'

Then she dived in, the conduit sparked even brighter. Then in a brilliant array of light it began to close.

In the aftermath the Angeon lay motionless on the mezzanine near the ceiling as Mitch drew closer. He hesitated before kneeling beside her. The Angeon was still breathing she managed a whisper, 'I don't want you to see me like this.'

Mitch whispered back, 'You still won't accept me.'

'Do you want to be with someone like this?' She asked.

'That is my choice,' he spoke.

'I don't even want to look at myself,' she remarked.

'That's something you're going to have to deal with,' he replied.

'I'm sorry,' she added.

Mitch let out a tear and kissed her on the forehead before she changed back. Saranon could sense several other wizards who had come to help. They moved her back into the normal hub of the Keep. She was aching all over. She was well enough to walk, but Mitch had insisted that she endure a bumpy ride while the wizards carried her out. He stayed by her side as some of the Palascene tried to get close and shooed them away with small gestures. She did not feel up to speaking with any Palascene, at least not for the moment. It was difficult to face Rachel as she saw her again. She had no reason to feel this way, though part of her did not like people seeing what she was.

Even though Rachel had not seen it firsthand, there was bound to be talk about it and for that she shied away from her friend. Rachel was professional as Saranon lay in silence mulling over her own thoughts. It was a delicate process one which seemed to take forever. She was expecting Rachel to say something, but she did not. The silence began to eat away at her until she cracked, 'Are there many casualties?'

'A few,' Rachel replied.

Saranon cringed of all the people that could be annoyed with her it had to be Rachel, 'What have I done?'

'You hurt Mitch. I thought you wanted the bond,' Rachel spoke.

She closed her eyes in thought, 'It would be nice to protect him from everything, but I can't.'

'He knows that,' Rachel relied.

Saranon wondered when Mitch had appointed Rachel as his spokesperson, or if her friend had taken it upon herself to do so.

She sat up and her heart pounded in her ears, 'This has nothing to do with Mitch. Now if it is all right with you, I would like to see him.'

'You can't, he's thinking of having the bond removed,' Rachel replied.

Saranon stood in dumbfounded silence she did not think she was that bad. Then she had just saved the Keep and perhaps that was too much for the both of them. 'That's his decision.'

With that she left and went back to her quarters. Some of Mitch's belongings were still there and she realised she would miss him a lot more than she thought she would. She sat down on the small couch perhaps it was for the best, she had enough trouble understanding wizards as it was.

There was a knock at the door, Mitch let himself in he sat down on the armchair near her looking awkward. 'I don't want to be shut out,' he said.

Saranon stood in front of him and held her arms out toward him. She could feel the change take over her body as the Angeon within her came alive, 'This is what I am.'

Mitch did not look away but he did not reach towards her either. She placed her hands by her side. 'Are you sure you want to be part of this?'

'I already am,' he said.

She changed back and Mitch held her close and whispered, 'I was offended because you shut me out.'

'I know,' was all she could think of.

He accepted her response, 'I've seen worse,' he said with a smile.

Saranon felt like running for the door would be a good thing to do right now. He read the expression on her face and was far from impressed. She stopped to wipe the tears from her eyes, 'I've got a bit of a problem I'm going to have to deal with Nathan.'

'That can wait until tomorrow,' he spoke.

Mitch stayed dragging out the comfy makeshift bed near the fireplace. Saranon was too tired to argue with him about the importance of privacy. As she had not grown up with much, it was more of a luxury. Talking of her friends made her think of Pennie, she had not heard from her for ages. She hoped Pennie was having more luck than she was, not that saving a Keep was not a massive achievement. Her friend had been stuck with a bunch of wizards. If Darkonian wizards were anything like the ones here, she could be having all sorts of problems. Then her friend had always been resourceful, perhaps everything was fine. She would have to find out after dealing with Nathan.

CHAPTER FIFTEEN

Complications with sorcerers

The morning brought the noise clambering to her door as Bianca burst through interrupting her sleep. 'Control that creature before I put it in the dungeon!'

Saranon looked at her still sleepy eyed as she rose from her comfy bed, 'I take it you mean Nathan.'

'Of course I mean Nathan who else do you think I mean, your dragon!'

'Well…' She started.

'Oh for the love of Normisia just fix it.' Bianca slammed the door behind her, but Saranon knew she was waiting for her.

She got herself dressed and made her way down with Mitch following close by. Everything appeared to be normal and Saranon thought that Bianca may have made a mistake. Then she entered the control room and shouted,

'Nathan!'

The Host turned around in surprise and ran off leaving a mess behind him. If she did not know better she would have sworn that the Host had been sabotaging the control room.

She turned to Bianca, the Palascene looked like she had woken up on the wrong side of the bed, 'Oh don't look at me, this is your mess.'

Bianca wandered off while Saranon tried to find a place to start. She could hear Nathan in the background and went to investigate.

The Host eyed her at floor level as he raised his head above the hard surface. The boards had been removed in a haphazard fashion as Nathan climbed out, and made his way toward her. The Host smiled as he swaggered forward, eyeing her. Saranon began to feel far less comfortable standing so close to him, as he approached. She still did not know what to make of him, but for some reason he had become her problem. She turned to peer down at the gaping hole holding the threaded conduits. The Host took the opportunity to place his arm around her. Without looking at him she put her hand up to his face and pushed him away.

'I thought you'd be happy to see me,' the Host spoke beside her.

She groaned in annoyance, it was going to be a long day. She jumped down into the shallow hole. The Host lay on the floor peering down over her shoulder as he rested his head on his arms. 'What makes you think you can do a better job than me?' He asked.

'I was hoping you could open the panel over there,' she pointed to the wall behind him.

'Oh, so now you need my help?' The Host made the remark seem rather boisterous and sat up, 'I don't think so.'

Saranon gaped in open astonishment as Nathan continued, 'First you can do something for me.'

'I beg your pardon,' she scowled in annoyance.

The Host had disregarded the fact that she was helping him.

He leaned down, and hauled her up to the floor as she eyed him with suspicion. This was not going according to plan and the Host took great enjoyment from changing the game. 'I want you to do something for me,' Nathan spoke as he reached over to the table. He removed the shiny surface and took out the broken fragments of a tiny power source.

'I would like three of these, in their original form,' Nathan for once was serious, and she could hear the Keep's words as he spoke.

She let out a heavy sigh, 'All right, but I need you to help.'

Nathan smiled as he let go of shattered pieces, and grabbed her hands swinging her around as he went. 'Nathan!' Saranon shouted with a sharp edge to her voice.

The Host did not seem to be listening as he continued, then just as she was unprepared, he let go. She tumbled back toward the open conduit as she placed her hands out to stop herself.

A massive surge ignited at the end of the conduit. Sparks flew everywhere as she stammered backwards into Nathan's grasp. As the haze cleared in the air from the smoke Saranon stared in utter disbelief. There, near the edge of the conduit, were five tiny shiny new power sources. As the smoke wafted down through the corridor she waited for someone to appear and yell at them, but no one came. The Host saw her gaze, and commented, 'I closed the door.'

The vents took the last of the smell away, but it still lingered in her clothes as she opened the windows. She asked, 'How did you know that would work?'

The Host was picking up the spare power sources, pocketing them for himself as he looked back, 'You only see me Nathan.'

Saranon wanted to say it was not true when she only saw the wizard. To her the Keep was a massive entity, and one body seemed rather small. She gazed out the window as the Host fixed the new power sources in place.

She was missing a glorious warm sunny day and she lingered a little longer before going back to help fix the control room. The Host had not stopped fiddling about, instead he had moved on to the next area. 'What are you doing?' She asked.

'Do you need to ask?' the Host did not look up.

Saranon peered over his shoulder and understood what he was doing, 'Do you need a hand?'

'I wouldn't say no,' he replied.

The two worked while for rest of the day, Bianca was nowhere to be seen, which was just as well. She did not feel like being sociable while recovering from saving the Keep. There was a strange silence between her and the Host, one where each other knew how close the danger had come.

It was soon getting late and Chelsea visited to see what they were doing, 'Aren't you going to eat? There's a nice big roast in the hall.'

Nathan looked up, 'That's sounds like a good reason to stop.'

He walked over to Chelsea who was not sure how to react. People had been avoiding Nathan all day, but she was not that type of person. Chelsea asked, 'I assume you still eat?'

'Yes,' he stated.

'Is it true that you don't need sleep?' Chelsea asked.

'I'm still human,' the Host replied.

Chelsea thought of more than a dozen other questions to ask the Host before they entered the hall. She noticed that Mitch had made himself at home on a table with his friends, so she sat with Chelsea. Nathan became a little restless and went to lounge near the fireplace. She did not take much notice until she heard shouting. As she turned to look a crowd had gathered near the fireplace and a high pitched scream rose above commotion. It sounded almost unnatural, then a faint wave of energy hummed down the walls, and she knew who it was.

She ran, and barged her way through as the circle of people closed tighter not wanting to let her through.

Saranon paused letting her sorcery flow inside. Without hesitation the crowd parted just in time for her to see Terrance holding Nathan to the ground. The Host struggled before her as he screamed again and she stood watching in silence. It pained her to watch as the sorcerer held the Host down, then she saw the hyrik emerge as Terrance held it out above the Host's head. Nathan's eyes grew wild as he pounded against the sorcerer to no avail.

Saranon went pale as the sorcerer placed it over Nathan's head, she was too shocked to watch, yet she could not look away. Terrance extended his sorcery to seal the hyrik in place, as it shrank, a stale smell wafted up through the air. Without warning the audience cleared away around her. She stood alone watching in horror. The hyrik began to melt and bubble as it evaporated. Before she could say anything, Terrance jumped out of the away, as the last remnants fell to the floor. She tried to work out what had happened and then a thought sank in.

The small group of Palascene stayed around the edge in a circle as if waiting, not knowing what had happened. She scowled in disbelief and held out her hand to the Host who was still shaking from his ordeal. She turned to face Terrance, 'You deserved that.'

With that she went to walk away, but she did not get far as the Palascene made it clear they wanted her to stay. She was not impressed. She had somehow taught the Keep how to remove a hyrik, but then the Palascene deserved as much. Terrance showed no signs of his attack on the Host as he stood before her. She had missed out on what started the argument and the Palascene were not pleased to see her. Another sorcerer tried to pull him away, but Terrance would not let it be.

Terrance stared her straight in the face, 'You were supposed to stop this creature.'

'You were supposed to stop the Dihan,' she replied with a sharp tone.

'We have accommodated you this far,' he stated with a firm edge.

Nathan moved closer and started shouting. Without turning she signalled for the Host to stop. To everyone else's surprise he obeyed and sat on the floor without making a sound. The two sorcerers glared at each other, the room had gone silent amidst their arguing. Terrance looked at the Host and Saranon knew what he was angry about, 'You want the Host for yourself.'

'Don't be absurd,' Terrance had had enough and turned to leave.

The Host spoke in a soft voice afterward, but it filled a void in the room, 'I'm sorry for getting you in trouble.'

She smiled, this time it was not Nathan's fault. She flumped down on the couch as she felt the last of her sorcery slip away and breathed a heavy sigh of relief. Saranon had her own complications without having to take on someone else's. The Host was not the least bit worried, as he enjoyed the rest of the evening. Although she did notice all the sorcerers in the room now stayed away, they were reluctant to encounter the Host again.

Terrance had left in a rage and there was not much

that Saranon could do about it. She returned to the control room after that, the sooner the place was fixed the better. Captain Mirshendy came to join them in the room as they worked into the night. The Captain had been good friends with Nathan and while she worked, the two managed to have a conversation. She had taken several panels off the wall and had managed to squeeze into the gap.

The Keep had shown her what to look for, although she was having trouble locating it, 'Nathan, I think we have a problem.'

The Host pulled off another panel where she had crawled to, and poked his head in, 'Ah, I see.'

The Captain took a closer look, 'That's not supposed to be like that.'

'Given my new fan club I think we should finish here first,' Saranon spoke with a hint of sarcasm.

The Captain was quite calm, 'You have a way of making friends.'

It was past midnight before they could run the first test. Saranon was starting to feel the lack of sleep in her muscles. Her body was still healing itself. Nathan fixed a few small glitches without any complaint and finally made his way to bed. She sat in silence looking at the results of their work with the Captain, 'You look like you want to say something.'

'You need to leave,' he spoke.

'What?' She asked.

'You were right about Terrance, you need to leave Redadere,' the Captain added.

'You had this planned?' She asked.

'You have served your purpose,' he responded.

'I think you know why I haven't received any contact from my friend Pennie?' She asked.

'It was for the best,' Captain Mirshendy said.

Saranon was not angry, but she was not impressed either. She was still in a grump when she ran out to meet Mitch and Katholomu in the courtyard. Mitch was already sitting in place he reached down and grabbed her hand pulling her up before she could say anything. The dragon took off with one giant leap disappearing into the warm night sky. He was quiet behind her, 'So what do you have to say for yourself?' She asked.

'You didn't want to speak with me,' he said.

'Very funny, I suppose you and the Captain had been planning this, she said.

'That's unfair,' he replied.

'As I recall you kidnapped me,' she retorted.

Mitch remained silent and Saranon could not understand why. After all it was she who deserved to be annoyed by what had happened. The magnificent creature they rode on made good time into Gosbin. Normisia's capital was much larger and far grander than Redadere. Katholomu descended toward one of the outer Keeps as the morning light rose to the east. As they came closer she grumbled when she realised it was another wizard stronghold, 'No. You're supposed to avoid wizards.'

It was too late the dragon was already touching down. Several wizards in familiar uniforms came scurrying out to meet them. 'This is your fault,' she said as she turned to Mitch.

He had a big grin on his face, 'Come on, you'd better get down.'

The dragon lowered himself to the ground so that they could descend much to Saranon's disgust, 'What did you do to my dragon?'

Mitch spoke, 'Saranon this is not the place.'

Before he could say anything else she slipped down, and went over to the greeting party. The man before her looked like Mitch and was well dressed. She was about to say something when he spoke first, 'I see you could not stay out of trouble.'

Evan stared straight at her as though expecting something. Without saying anything further he beckoned them to follow him inside. As they passed by the decorated walls she turned to Mitch and whispered, 'You gave that up?'

'Yes,' he whispered back.

Then she asked Evan. 'Are you sure you're related to Mitch?'

Evan looked at his brother then back at Saranon, 'Yes.'

As the two brothers made polite conversation she peered out of the window in the small cosy room. She looked down to Katholomu who was taking no notice of her. She curled up in the chair and before realising it fell fast asleep Mitch woke her up, and she came too with a start, 'Did I miss anything?'

Mitch smiled, 'No.'

She could only just contain her excitement when she heard her friend Pennie was visiting. For now she had to wait, which was completely incomprehensible. As she thought of Pennie and how long it had been since they had seen each other. Saranon tried not to fidget, but the two wizards were beginning to bore her. As she looked closer she noticed Evan was wearing a familiar symbol on a small chain near his belt. It was the same mark from Ollanthia, a warped tear drop pattern and she wondered what he was doing wearing a Darkonian symbol.

The small object glistened in the sunlight, Evan noticed her staring, and did not say anything. As they left she had a chance to ask Mitch, 'How well do you know your brother?'

'That's a strange question,' Mitch commented.

'He was wearing a familiar symbol,' she spoke.

'We are on good terms with the Asdenard,' he knew what she was referring to.

She was not so sure about Mitch's answer, but did not press the matter further, 'So where is Pennie?'

Mitch was about to speak when her friend came running toward her. It was like a dream as they embraced so far from home. Tears escaped down her cheek and Pennie was the same. He had disappeared as they ran off out into the warm open air.

Saranon took a moment to compose herself wiping her face, Pennie looked a lot more relaxed, 'So how are you?'

'I'm fine. In fact I'm better than fine my health is

good.'

'How?' Saranon exclaimed.

'Could you believe it the Normisian's cured me,' Pennie said.

'Really,' she was astonished.

Pennie smiled and Saranon felt all the sorrow inside her trying to swell up again. They had been through some tough times and this was the longest they had been apart. 'Do you think I'll be able to return someday?' Saranon asked.

'Well if Jacob has anything to do with it, I would think so,' Pennie replied.

'How is he?' She asked.

'Why don't you ask him yourself?' Pennie spoke.

She was flabbergasted, 'They let him in Normisia.'

Pennie roared with laughter, 'He didn't have any trouble.'

Pennie had a hundred and one questions about her journey which was fine, except for the fact that it felt more like an interrogation. Her friend was a stickler for detail and any attempts to fob Pennie off, were met with a stern disapproving look. The hot afternoon sun pelted down between the trees near the outer rim of Zaidek. The great Keep for all its glory, was smaller than Greddin. The building above ground was similar, though it was in much better condition. The wizards kept a close eye on them without giving away too many signs. Saranon thought to herself that not much had changed. Off in the distance she could make out Jacob's tall slender frame, he looked as though he was in no hurry to meet her.

Pennie looked much better than she did last time, though the illness had taken its toll. Jacob was not hard to find, he was making polite conversation with Mitch much to Saranon's amazement. He looked different to the way she remembered, perhaps because so much had happened. The wind played in his hair and along his coat, but his eyes stayed focused. He looked out of place in the manicured gardens that swept at their feet, then so did she.

'I didn't think you were allowed out?' She asked.

He smiled as she screwed up her face in disgust. 'Did you think I would not find you?' Jacob spoke.

'I thought you didn't want to see me again,' Saranon remarked.

'I said you needed to leave Darkonia,' he replied.

'But…'

'You misunderstood,' he interrupted.

Mitch was trying not to crack up laughing she could sense it, but his lips remained unmoved. Pennie seemed not to notice, 'Now are you going to introduce me to your companion?'

'Ah yes, well you see it's like… this is Mitch,' Saranon motioned with her hands towards the towering wizard.

'My name is Mitchell Kregner,' with great sensitivity he reached down and kissed Pennie on the hand.

Her friend was taken aback by the gesture, 'Well you must be a special person to place your faith in her.'

'Yes,' he replied.

She opened her mouth to say something, but thought

better of it as Mitch stared at her. As he continued to charm her old friend she took the opportunity to take Jacob aside. He peered over his shoulder then back, 'You chose a Normisian?'

'It was an accident,' she snapped at him.

She kicked a lose pebble from the path in frustration then looked up at him, 'You've changed.'

'No,' he commented.

As Saranon left, her eyes were heavy with exhaustion as the sun began to set behind the hills. Zaidek was placed to look over most of Gosbin. The city dwarfed Redadere in size. The elegance of Gosbin's grand buildings far outshone the smaller city. Dinner was a strange experience, she had not stayed long, even though the wizards were happy to make casual conversation. It was small talk about nothing and Evan did not seem at all interested in answering any of her questions. She left Mitch who was relaxing and catching up with old friends, as she wandered down the hall toward her room.

'Saranon,' whispered Pennie from somewhere around the bend.

'What are you doing?' she whispered back.

'Hush,' her friend replied.

Saranon just wanted to go to sleep, even though Pennie would not be impressed. The two of them made their way through the labyrinth of pathways inside the Keep.

Pennie had mastered the art of snooping a long time ago, but she was not so light on her feet. Several times her friend gave her a cross stare for making too much noise. In the wizards' Keep they could almost conceal themselves. Wizards by nature detested the thought of not being able to know everything that was happening.

When they finally reached their destination her friend knelt down so that Saranon could take a peak. She asked, 'What are they doing?'

'I don't know, but it's a problem,' Pennie whispered.

'Why is that?' She asked.

'Because they want you,' Pennie replied

'Nonsense,' she remarked.

Pennie was in no mood to mess around, 'They will not let us leave.'

Saranon was not impressed, 'We can talk about this in the morning.'

'I'm trying to help,' her friend remarked.

Saranon could not see the sinister side of a bunch of sorcerers hanging around in a wizards Keep. After all, that was what she was doing, and besides the Keep felt fine. Pennie was one for worrying too much over nothing. In morning she would entertain her friend's idea and find out what was happening.

CHAPTER SIXTEEN

Partial acceptance

Saranon woke up with the bustle of everyday life, she looked around the room it felt empty without Mitch. She would have to face Pennie, it was a dreary thought, but she had brushed her friend aside last night. In fact she had been doing that ever since Tasha's death. She did not think Pennie was able to lead their small group which was now down to two. Perhaps they needed to recruit some new members? No sooner than the thought had entered her mind than a sorcerer close to her age ran toward her, he was Darkonian.

Richard grabbed her by the arm, 'Pennie's in trouble.'

'Hang on, what do you mean?' She asked.

'She did not return last night, when I went to look for her I heard that she had been taken,' he spoke in haste.

Saranon thought that Richard was not brave. The

more she heard the more she realised that Pennie had stumbled across something, 'You leave it to me.'

'We're wasting time,' he responded.

Richard followed her to where Evan and Mitch were. 'I do not see Pennie,' she spoke as she faced Evan.

'Did you think there would be no price for her recovery?' Evan commented.

'That was paid with Greddin,' she remarked.

'Ah, but you were the one who almost destroyed it. The Palascene are willing to teach you if you accept the hyrik that way we both get what we want,' Evan spoke in a calm tone.

Saranon hated his smile, but she knew that being a prisoner would cost much more. With a sudden jolt the Keep stopped. Right on cue the occupants of the Keep started going into a panic. She signalled to Mitch, 'I think it's time to leave.'

Mitch gave her a worried look as he obeyed they walked through the chaos to where Katholomu was. The majestic dragon lowered his head and stared her in the eye as he spoke one word, 'Coward.'

The word shook the ground like thunder making Saranon stop in her tracks. She wanted to argue with the massive beast, but dragons were known for being stubborn. It was cold, she looked up to see the weather had changed from calm to stormy grey and in her heart she knew it was time. The dragon had brought her here for a reason and now it was time. Her former self fell away in an instant vanishing in the cold wind which swept around her. It was a small price to pay to be who she was. This time it was Evan who came running flanked by wizards. Tiny pieces of ground began to crumble, falling away fast to create a rift between her and the wizards. It spread either side around one section of the Keep.

'Saranon you can't do this,' Mitch was terrified of what he was witnessing.

'Yes I can. Tell your brother to back down, and I will restore the Keep,' the Angeon spoke.

For a moment in the noise that roared around them Mitch remained silent, without speaking he did what he was asked. 'You have what you want,' he replied.

She kept her word, but did not change back. Instead she walked up to the wizards who fell back until she came face to face with Evan.

She caressed his face with the back of her fingers, and whispered so that no one else could hear. 'If you think I could take a Keep this size with such little effort you are mistaken.'

Evan did not reply so she made her way back into the Keep. Mitch interrupted, 'So the weather is not your doing?'

'You do not recognise your own Keep?' She answered.

Evan was not convinced, 'Are you sure it was the Keep?'

'Yes,' she replied.

They moved inside and Katholomu followed them in a rush, as the rain broke into a torrent. Saranon changed back as she looked out the window in disgust. The rain could be a soothing sound, but this was something different. Mitch shared a moment with his brother before joining her, 'This is how the Palascene punish those who go against them. If you want to help you need to make amends.'

To her surprise Pennie came running up to her, 'Can someone please tell me what's going on?'

'Where have you been?' She could not believe her friend would vanish.

Pennie shook some dirt off her clothes, 'I had to wait so I wouldn't be spotted.' She looked up at Saranon, 'Oh no, I know that look.'

Pennie waited for Saranon's reply, 'We need Bianca.'

'Oh no,' her friend responded.

Saranon stared at her friend, 'All right then, you figure it out.'

'But Bianca doesn't like me,' Pennie blurted out.

'I have faith in you,' Saranon replied.

'Oh no, you're not leaving this one up to me,' Pennie exclaimed.

Evan stepped in, 'I hate to interrupt, but if you could assist we would consider it a favour in kind for saving your life.'

Pennie knew what he meant, 'I will get to it then.'

Saranon wanted to follow her although Pennie could manage on her own. Before long she found herself with only Mitch for company.

'You did not ask before you threatened my brother,' he spoke.

Saranon was going to make a snide remark, then

thought better of it. 'So I'm expected to be civilised?' She exclaimed.

'That's not what I meant,' he remarked.

The rain gushed through the night the Keep muffled the sound, though she knew it was there as she drifted in and out of sleep. Mitch could not sleep either, 'Is there any reason why you asked for Bianca?'

'There's something odd about her,' she answered.

'You embarrassed my brother,' Mitch was not going to let the matter be.

'I'm a sorceress, that's what I do best,' she responded still half asleep.

As she rested, Saranon could feel Mitch staring at her. It made her feel uncomfortable, but there was nothing she could do to reassure him. The wizards had backed down and now she had to live with that. The morning was silent as she peered out the window to a bright clear day. She looked down and saw Bianca approaching with her entourage behind her. Pennie burst into the room. 'Saranon, Bianca is a master.'

'No wonder she looked down at me,' she commented.

Mitch invited himself into the conversation, 'She's too young?'

'You mean like me?' Saranon asked.

'You are an anomaly.'

'Hey,' Saranon noticed that he had developed an attitude since being at Zaidek. She was not sure if it was her or Evan who was causing it.

As if reading her mind Mitch gave her a wide cheesy

grin. She did not like to admit it, but it was nice to have someone else around.

Mitch remained silent though she knew he was not impressed. They watched as the rest of the procession was led inside. As much as Mitch wanted her to go and kept on staring at her as a reminder, she knew it was not a good idea. She hung back lulled by the distant hum of the Keep, and the sun shone down on the balcony where they stood. The wizards made the occasional glance up at her from the courtyard, where they hurried about below.

It was a waiting game and one Mitch was not comfortable with. The former soldier had been built for fighting and underneath the relaxed pose, he was frustrated. He finally broke his composure and sat on the balcony next to Saranon, 'What are you expecting from this?'

'A little leeway,' she answered.

'I still think you should have gone with Pennie,' he spoke.

The two sat chatting away while the world went on around them.

'They make a wonderful couple,' Bianca's voice hailed from the courtyard below.

Mitch looked down and knew that now was a goodtime to Keep quiet. Saranon was about to say something. 'There is no need to say anything. You are now linked to the Keep, which means you will not be able to leave,' Bianca smiled and then left.

'What does she mean?' She glared at Pennie as she jumped down off the balcony, in front of her friend in the courtyard.

'This way is best for all of us,' her friend answered.

Saranon ran off and Pennie yelled behind her, 'No don't, if you try to break it you will end up..!'

Her blood was boiling with anger, Mitch was right she should not have left Pennie in charge. She sprinted to the end of the Keep's territory, and felt the link. Pennie was right, but then so was she. She held out her hands as her energy surged through, as it seared against the link she could feel it weaken. She plunged herself through, it made a terrible breaking noise which bled back into the Keep.

As she opened her eyes, things looked normal enough, so she made her way down to the city it was silent. She moved around the street which lay empty, something was not right. She moved through the walls and into a building, then into another, and another. They were all silent with no people or animals and no sign of life except the vegetation which covered the landscape beyond. She wandered down to the shore where the water was black, this world was not real.

She stepped forward and as her foot plunged into the water, it subsided leaving a gap. The waves continued to wash ashore as though nothing had happened, whatever this world was she was not sure she wanted to be in it. The sand looked fine as she made her way back to the dune and strode along to cave at the far end. As she approached she could make out a small makeshift table. She picked up a book, but when she looked down at the writing she could not make it out. The words changed fleeting in and out, not wanting to make sense.

A breeze travelled through the air sweeping the papers off the table and into the air. As Saranon tried to catch them they disappeared, melting into the pebbles along the dune. As she stood up a figure appeared, waiting at near the end of the cave. She walked closer, and realised it was Tasha dressed in the finery that would have been hers had she lived. The two girls stood side by side and Tasha spoke first, 'I cannot stay long, you are in a different phase that is why you cannot see anyone.'

Saranon went to say something and Tasha answered, 'I am Tasha's spirit nothing more. The Palascene have committed a crime, they must know the meaning of sacrifice and you will bring this to them. Kill the boy, but leave the girl. Do you understand?'

'Yes,' she replied.

'The boy has chosen the path of destruction, he must be stopped,' Tasha explained. 'You can make your own way back.'

'What?' She asked in astonishment.

'You know how,' and with that Tasha faded into oblivion, leaving her alone.

Saranon was still stuck with no idea of how to get out perhaps the answer would be with the Palascene? Their Keep was further back from the coast, facing Elspy River, which swept through the middle of Normisia. The enormity of the unknown began to sag down on her shoulders as the distance in this phase made no sense. She reached the Keep in no time at all. The place was becoming creepy as she thought she could see shadows moving in her peripheral vision. Aneeda Keep shimmered as she entered into the strange world she reached out her hand. She touched the wall sensing all the life that ran through the Keep.

Something connected in her mind and the noise around her burst into her ears with a burning sensation after the silence. She held onto Aneeda trying to make sense of it all, a voice sprang out of the darkness, 'Are you all right?'

She turned around and Rianna gasped with recognition then ran away. Saranon stayed where she was, while her mind caught up with her body. The sorceress, Rianna returned with a blanket and Saranon realised she was sweating as she wrapped herself in it. Rianna's eyes were kind so she followed her to a warm lounge area.

Rianna watched her in silence as Saranon downed a pitcher of water before she stopped for a break. From the corner of her eye she saw Bianca enter the room and sit beside her mother. 'You embarrassed me,' was all Bianca said.

She was still groggy, 'It was…it was not your decision.'

She rubbed her eyes and put down her empty glass. Bianca glanced at her mother, Rianna, 'As a member of the Palascene…'

'No, no, you are supposed to lead. Tell me, what is your decision?' She interrupted.

Bianca remained silent and so Saranon walked over to her holding out something she had kept hidden in her hand. She passed it to Bianca and said, 'You know where to find me,' then left.

She heard Rianna gasp and Bianca ran after Saranon, 'Please tell me where you got this?'

Bianca held the small sacra seal in her hand, and Saranon stopped, 'I made it.'

'But you can't, you're not…' Bianca began.

'I'm not what?' She asked.

'You are not trained. Wait, stay for a while,' Bianca pleaded.

She was fast running out of options and with a sinking feeling agreed. As much as she could put on a show, she could not sustain her ability for long and at the end of the day Bianca was just one Palascene. In a way she knew Pennie was right, though she hated being trapped. Bianca smiled, 'I think you should return to Zaidek, I will meet you there. Try not to cause any trouble.'

Saranon knew it was a close escape and was ready for a rest from all the excitement, 'I will try my best.'

'Oh! By the way, your dragon is waiting outside,' Bianca said.

It was her turn to look surprised as she followed the Palascene to the courtyard. Bianca strode next to her and reached out to touch the magnificent creature. 'Now, straight to Zaidek and I expect you to Keep an eye on Saranon.'

Katholomu bowed his head much to her annoyance. She clambered up and without hesitation they were away. She whispered in his ear, 'Whose side are you on?'

The dragon made a rumbling sound like a stifled

laugh which reverberated through his belly and they began to descend.

The flight was over too soon, and she saw familiar faces rushing out to greet her as they landed. She clambered down with deflated excitement as Pennie gave her a worried hug, and spoke, 'Please don't do that again.'

Before she had time to answer, Pennie whisked her inside into a small cosy room and gave her a stern look, 'What did Tasha tell you?'

Saranon almost fell out of chair in disbelief as her friend continued, 'The wizards know, they told the Palascene. It's the only reason you haven't been pummelled out of existence. Now tell me.'

'Kill the boy, but leave the girl, she wants to punish the Palascene,' she spoke.

Pennie went quiet and put her head in her hands. Then after a brief moment recovered, 'Why do you always have to make things difficult?'

Saranon wandered off, being told off like a small child by two people in one day was more than enough. Zaidek was content whirring away in the back of her mind. She had the distinct impression that not much surprised it.

She walked back along the top of the internal courtyard retracing her steps. She could see the wizards training below. She made out two familiar faces Captain Mirshendy and Mitch. They appeared to be completely in their element and she felt like the odd one out. She was in no doubt that the wizards trained hard, compared to someone like her. They made it look easy, that was no small feat. Saranon cringed at the thought that she was staring down at the same people who had held her captive, not the nicest thought. The smell of old sweat wafted up and she frowned in disgust. Better leave them be, she thought.

'So are you going to come down and join us?' Captain Graddon asked.

She broke out of her self-absorbed thought. She stared down at the wizard standing by Captain Mirshendy's side. Jerald answered her look of dismay, 'This is Captain Hugh Graddon and the stairs are over there.' The Captain pointed.

She mumbled out loud as she descended, 'Why would I want to join you?'

Being down in the stench did not appeal to her as Captain Graddon replied, 'Because you are disrupting my officers.'

She was about to say 'yes I know', but the Captain continued. 'Now over there is the equipment.'

Without looking, Captain Graddon threw a staff Saranon's way, she fumbled and managed to catch it. She looked up at Captain Mirshendy with pleading eyes, but all the Captain could do was smile. 'Now you need to get into these.' Hugh pulled out some gear that matched her size, 'You can get changed over in there.'

She felt like shouting 'I am not a wizard', but she did not think it would do any good. So she went into the ladies change room and tried to find a corner to hide in. The whole thing seemed ridiculous and she almost tripped over twice as she mumbled under her breath.

She looked at herself in the mirror and felt ridiculous as she shrugged her shoulders. She placed her belongings in a sova bag then picked up the staff, this was not her day. Saranon grumbled as Mitch led her into the centre of a circular space, off to the side of the other wizards' training. Before she was ready, he clouted her side with his staff, the impact knocked the wind out of her lungs as she jumped out of the way. She was about to say 'that's not fair', but he moved so quick she struggled to keep up. He made her feeble attempts appear haphazard as he managed to strike her again. This time she was not impressed, using her energy to jump up and bounce out of the way, hitting him from behind with her staff.

Mitch did not flinch as he responded in kind he was not going to let her be. As he side stepped she managed to catch him off-guard. Yet the small victory was short-lived as his staff fell across her back with a dull thud. She was thankful they were not fighting for real, even though it still hurt. He caught her again and she only just managed to strike out in time to stop another blow. Mitch was enjoying the struggle, as her temper flared underneath the surface. He could be infuriating and she jumped out of the way.

Saranon was beginning to tire of the exercise, that and Mitch was winning. She thrust her way toward him and he managed to fend off every blow. He smiled in return at her annoyance as she leaped toward him, and he struck her again. She was not going to win and conceded as she held up her hand to stop. She was exhausted, as she turned to find they had become the centre of attention to a waiting crowd.

Captain Graddon was about to pat her on the back and she moved to the side. Jerald saw part of her back glimpsing between her trousers and top, 'Where did you get that? Mitch you didn't tell me about that.'

'I do not get that personal,' Mitch replied.

He was not impressed by the accusation as he stood close by.

Captain Mirshendy examined Saranon's back as she was starting to panic. She half whimpered, 'Mitch.'

Mitch leaned over, 'Ah, sir?'

Captain Mirshendy realised how big a fuss he had made, 'Most people don't get a scar like that, and live to tell the tale.'

Saranon gave Mitch a filthy look as he tried to cover his tracks. He grabbed her hand and whispered, 'Sorry about that.'

The two practised in the courtyard until it was time to pack up, she could not wait to get back into her own clothes. Mitch patted her on the shoulder with a hint of approval she was still annoyed at him for showing off. He was more than happy to gloat as several wizards praised him, which annoyed her even more. She could not wait to leave as she wiped the sweat from her brow.

As Mitch approached she rushed out to hand her gear back, 'Where do I put these?'

'No, you keep them for tomorrow. If you want I'll wash them?'

Saranon handed them over she gave him a stern look,

'What do you mean tomorrow?'

He smiled, 'You will be coming tomorrow.'

She did not like being ordered around least of all by Mitch.

Captain Mirshendy came up beside them, 'I'm afraid he's right, you can fight so you can train.'

'But…' She began.

The Captain came close, 'Do you know how lucky you are? You bring fear into the hearts of many, you will train with us.'

Saranon was about to burst into tears as she looked at Mitch. Then ran all the way up to her quarters and flung herself on the bed. The sun was just starting to set as she wiped her hand across the tears on her face.

She struggled, it had all been too much as the memory of Tasha clung on. All she wanted to do was run away, but she could not. She wanted to scream and instead she was left having to deal with the Cryzinelan wizards. She wondered if the Palascene had asked the wizards to look after her just to give them something to do, instead of annoying them. This was definitely not how she thought it would be, and sighed. Yet again she was stuck in a wizard's Keep.

Tea would be ready but she did not feel like going, she could always go down later. There was a knock at the door Mitch came in with a bag full of clean clothes, and something to eat. 'Did you get into trouble too?' She asked.

'Nothing I can't handle,' he replied.

He came over and sat at the end of the bed, 'We need all the help we can get.'

Mitch's words were not comforting.

Saranon stared up at the ceiling, 'Did I take all this on with you?'

'I'm afraid so,' he smiled.

'Wizards should come with a warning label, no offence,' she exclaimed.

'I hate to tell you, but sorcerers usually don't bond wizards,' he replied.

She wanted to say more and stopped herself. The last thing she wanted to do at the moment was end up in a discussion over something he knew more about than her. She resigned herself to the fact that she was not going to win the argument.

The bruises from the exercise taunted her as she tried to rest. Yet for all her scattered thoughts, it did not take long before she fell into a deep sleep. The only image that entered her dream was that of the black water at the edge of the beach. It lapped away with the pull of the waves breaking along the shore. There was no sign of Tasha, yet she could feel her friend's presence as though she had only just left. In that moment she waited and every moment felt as though it would last forever.

CHAPTER SEVENTEEN

The trouble with wizards

The place still smelled as Saranon walked through the courtyard, even though it was just a memory. It smelled of roses if that was possible. It was early in the morning, and Mitch had left over an hour ago. She could tell that he was content spending time with Evan. Pennie was busy as usual she had changed since Saranon had left Darkonia. Her friend was still the same, things had just become complicated. Captain Graddon saw her, 'If you keep standing around I'll find something for you to do.'

'I'm avoiding cleaning my dragon,' she commented.

'Ah, well I can always find something worse,' the Captain responded.

'I'll be fine,' she replied as she rushed off.

She had been neglecting Katholomu and went down to the pens to get some peace and quiet. The wizards took great pride in looking after their dragons and the place was kept as clean as could be. She was not sure what to make of Captain Graddon, he was different to Jerald. The fact that she was a sorceress did not seem to bother him. Katholomu, otherwise known as 'Kat' spotted her and sprang into life popping his giant head around the corner. The dragon was in a playful mood and when she stepped close he moved with astounding grace. He came back and rubbed himself up against Saranon before taking off again.

The game continued for some time before Kat rolled over, as if playing dead, wanting his tummy rubbed. His fur and scales were ratty and covered in grime. Katholomu's black colour hid his love of running through caves, and rolling around in the dirt. She groaned as she rolled up her sleeves, and grabbed a soft scrubbing brush. The dragon thought the whole process was fun as he lay there purring away half asleep. The murky water escaped down one of the many drains. As Katholomu stood up he showed off his elegant markings that stated his claim to fine breeding. In a seductive manner for any dragon that may be looking in his direction. 'That's a fine dragon you have,' Gabriel spoke as she patted Kat's glistening damp fur.

Saranon said, 'Thank you. You may want to remove your hand.'

Gabriel looked puzzled, but did as she suggested. She dried the dragon with her sorcery he looked content so she clambered down, 'I'm Saranon.'

'I know who you are. Captain Graddon is my uncle, and I've been helping with Katholomu.'

The great dragon moved over to a nice dry nook that fitted his size then curled up to sleep, with one eye open.

'Your uncle isn't scared of me?' She commented.

'His wife is a sorceress. Uncle Hugh says that it takes a great person to master a marmoz.' Gabriel spoke.

'I don't know about master, a pain in the neck is more like it,' she remarked.

The dragon smiled in reply as the girls wandered over to some of the dragon handlers having a break. It was getting late with the darkness dancing on the edge of the well-lit walls, while the stars were hidden behind the clouds.

'So you're the one that tamed Mitch,' Owen spoke over mouthfuls of a hot brew of coffee, the smell wafted up through the room.

Saranon was taken by surprise, 'I didn't tame him.'

Gabriel laughed. 'The rebellious son of the great Haiden Kregner and now you've placed Mitch in a higher position.'

'Have I?' Saranon was more than a little confused it did not make sense that bonding could give a wizard status.

Gabriel smiled at her bewildered look there were a lot of things she did not understand. At times she only just managed to muddle her way through. Owen and Gabriel seemed genuine enough, so she stayed until it was time to get some rest. The company was a nice relief from all the disapproval that carried her down.

Saranon made her way to bed trying not to disturb Mitch as she tiptoed past. 'It's all right I'm awake,' his voice travelled behind her in the dark.

'Sorry,' she had woken him a few times with her odd hours, 'Did you want to spend time with your kin?'

'Are you trying to get rid of me?' he asked.

'No, I just thought that you would want to spend time with your family.'

She could see that Mitch was thinking about it. He answered by rolling over and going to sleep.

The day was young and the Palascene had organised schooling for her. She was suspicious of the convenient way her schooling was organised. It ended in the early afternoon, when Captain Graddon expected her to take part in training. At first Pennie had been dismissive of the whole coincidence of the arrangement. Before admitting she had known for a while. Her friend had glued herself to the library and the many dull texts within.

Pennie had become obsessed with an Angeon who died more than two hundred years earlier. The great Zeralden Hadenvar whose legend lived on in mythical proportions. Saranon preferred to disassociate herself with the image. In comparison her life appeared meagre and dull. For once she was quite content to resign herself to having her life dictated. Beforehand the mere thought would have sent shivers down her spine, but for once things were as close to fine as they could be.

She was helping Pennie in the library when the lights of the Keep dimmed for a moment. Her friend could see the look on her face, 'It's nothing to worry about.'

She was in the middle of drawing cartoon figures of

her fellow classmates, when Mitch stared over at her handy work. 'I see you're ready to go on duty.'

'What?' She remarked.

Pennie did not look at all surprised, 'Captain Graddon's been training you so you can help.'

He placed a friendly hand on Saranon's shoulder, 'Come on, we'll be late.'

Mitch could not wipe the smile from his face as they walked down to training. With each step she was getting a little more agitated. The exercise did not help her mood and it went far too quick as she went with him along to the equipment room. It was a large hub of excitement as people were either gearing up, or returning items. No one seemed bothered by the fact that some of the items were rather deadly. He came back with a pile of gear including some garments for her. 'Oh no, I'm not wearing that,' Saranon exclaimed.

'It will help keep you safe,' he stated.

Sienna came up to greet them. She was a roughly beautiful woman with a hard edge to her features, 'Dressing her up won't make any difference.'

Mitch's eyebrows were starting to drop in an unimpressed look, 'Fine you decide.'

'It's okay,' Sienna hustled Saranon over to where the sorcerers' garments were kept.

At the end of the day she had enough experience for the glamour of working to have worn thin.

She bypassed a heap of items that looked too elaborate to withstand daily wear. Then headed straight for some hardy items, and yanked them off the rack. 'I don't think you'll need that,' Sienna tried grabbing one of the items as Saranon moved sideways and ducked around.

She had worn similar gear before in Darkonia when she travelled alone. It had served her well and she was not one to be concerned with fashion.

As she finished she strode out to skim past the weaponry and sized up a couple pieces before taking her pick. She turned toward Mitch, 'I'm ready.'

'Okay,' was all Mitch could manage as he prepared himself.

'Hey, you've…' Sienna took a closer look. 'I was going to say you put it on the wrong way, but you haven't.'

Saranon did not know what all the fuss was about. If the gear was not meant to be worn, it would not be there in the first place. She made her way with Mitch to the group and said nothing.

It all seemed straight forward as she kept up pace with Mitch. Patrolling was something that stirred the senses in her blood, but this time she stayed in line. She felt she had nothing to prove, except showing that she could be part of a team. For a while she had been part of a team in the detention camps, but that was different. Now she strode in a mix of pride as the warm night air set about with a stagnant stillness around the streets. She felt her palms tingle with the energy that was burning inside. Mitch could feel it too they were getting close. Then everything went cold, an officer went to look inside one of the buildings and Mitch stood behind near the door way.

There were muffled sounds from within and the wizards sprang through the walls.

Mitch hesitated, waiting for Saranon. She stood outside in the silence holding his stare then walked through the door. She could sense movement off in the distance, but it was all happening too fast. Her palms had gone numb with the cold, yet the air around them was warm. This time she had no urge to fight, this was a family home and something was wrong. Her mood was reflected in Mitch's face and she saw a couple of the wizards in the shadows. They remained almost hidden as if waiting for someone, waiting for her. She opened the door, and walked in. The stench hit her hard, but that was the least of her concerns as she looked down, she knew they were too late.

What she had sensed earlier, had left before they arrived. The body was covered and there was not much they could do. Captain Graddon spoke up afterward, 'You will have to move quicker,' he said as he passed Saranon by.

They moved on in silence leaving the place behind. As they moved on, there were a few of the normal squabbles that needed breaking up. Outside the Lady Jade Inn an older man had been beaten by a couple of youths. For some reason the Captain seemed right at home dragging the youths away. They stopped and had a short break back at the station listening to the drunken youths shouting in the distance.

The Captain kept a steady pace moving around, as a few strangers were given a friendly warning. The rest of the night was peaceful, much to her delight. It had not felt like a lot of work, but the sweat had stuck to her hair. As she was back in the safety of the Keep, she took off the heavy garments and jumped when she saw something move on her hand. There was a gale of laughter behind her as it dawned on her that the wizards had played a trick. She glared at Mitch who joined in before storming off to get cleaned up. He cornered her as she left, 'I'll be staying down in the dorm tonight, is that okay?'

'I suppose so,' she replied.

Saranon was still fuming and stubbed her toe while clambering up the stairs. In retrospect the night had been a disaster, she had not been able to keep up, the wizards moved in a completely different way. In reality she had held them back, it was not a good start, but then was it what she wanted? Pennie was too absorbed and had been quite content not to fill her in on what was happening. In Darkonia the long nights travelling had been relaxing and thrilling. Here everybody was happy to make fun of her, perhaps it was time to move on. The thought lingered as the warm night air lulled her off to sleep.

In some ways the night had drowned her sorrows as Saranon watched Mitch wander off with a group downstairs. He could look after himself, so that was the least of her worries. Zaidek had been silent since her arrival and she was beginning to feel a little claustrophobic. The Keep had extensive grounds which led into the open countryside. She hurried down to find Katholomu in the yard already waiting. This time the dragon needed no encouragement. Kat bounded off the ground to the surprise of several onlookers. The coolness of the breeze swept against her cheeks. Everything looked so peaceful from above, in stark contrast to the turmoil welling up inside. She rode the dragon down near the edge of the city that circled in Zaidek's wake.

The great waters of the Elspy River stretched down before her. Katholomu took a flying leap into the water and pulled out a large fish from the deep. Saranon sheltered herself from the wet barrage, as any attempt to remain hidden, faded away. The dragon seemed completely oblivious as he purred his way through the meal. She heard a rustle behind her and Gabriel came rushing down the hill toward her. 'Glad to see you've taken Kat out, he was getting restless.'

'What are you doing here?' She asked.

'This is a dragon stop, come on,' Gabriel gestured.

Katholomu followed as she walked at a slower pace. She was greeted by a temporary camp site with several dragons smaller than her own.

Owen was among the group, 'So the Captain let you out?'

Saranon's mood soured. 'It was only a joke,' he remarked.

'That's been happening a lot lately,' she wanted to shrug it off, but every time it hurt a little.

'Did you want to fly with us down further to Furly's Gates?' Owen asked.

She had heard of the great stone walls rising either side of the river. She wanted to be left alone, but Katholomu was already nudging her from behind, 'Oh, all right.'

The dragon nuzzled her hand with eager anticipation before she jumped on. It was strange flying in formation, though there was no effort on her part since Kat was doing all the work.

At least there was one consolation the day was beautiful and silent except for the breeze. A buzzing came from her talik destroying her thoughts it was Gabriel, 'What do you think of the view?'

It all looked the same to Saranon and she tried to sound enthused. The long grass wafted its smell up to greet her nose in a strong blast of wind. She sneezed into the dragon's fur as he landed, causing him to groan with dissatisfaction. She gathered herself before staring up, Furly's Gates looked much bigger now that she was on the ground.

'Come on,' Gabriel was already ahead of her, and she ran to catch up. 'You don't use much sorcery?'

She looked up puzzled as she caught up. It had never occurred to her that it was unusual, 'I guess not.'

'If you were one of the Palascene we'd have trouble getting you to stop,' Gabriel spoke.

Saranon did not know what to say to that and so kept plodding on. 'Hey, are you listening to me?' Gabriel asked.

She cringed, 'Yes.'

'So why don't you use your sorcery?' Gabriel asked.

Owen interrupted, 'If Saranon wants to tell you she will. Do you want to see the caves?'

Gabriel's stubborn look changed to excitement,

'Come on it'll be fun.'

Gabriel dashed in front of them and walked through the wall. Saranon hesitated. Owen held out his hand to her and she followed his lead.

Inside was dry and airy. Wizard lights had been placed throughout and lit up as they moved around. The place had been well used with little chips and dents marking its lifespan. A short distance in, the markings on the wall became clearer and Saranon could not keep her eyes off the ceiling. 'I thought you would like it,' Gabriel pronounced in a loud voice.

She reached out sensing the place, it was filled with a great richness. Something sharp came to her mind and she pulled back, 'What was this place?'

'It's where the Cryzinelan hid during the great invasion,' Gabriel replied.

The pictures on the walls fascinated her. She heard a sound through the walls, it was Katholomu, 'I have to go.'

'I'm sure it's nothing,' Gabriel commented.

'I'm sorry, but I have to go,' she replied.

Saranon rushed out through the maze to see another dragon attacking Katholomu. It blocked her from getting close. She tried to restrain it, but she could not.

She could feel the energy inside her grow as she hurled a blast which spiralled through the air, warping as it went. The dragon screamed in terror as the blast hit its side sending it flying. Knocking out several trees as it went, before disappearing. She ran over to Kat and breathed a sigh of relief when she saw his wounds were only superficial. The dragons gaze turned toward Mitsy, Gabriel's shazel dragon. The dragon had marks on her face and stomach, they were not life threatening, but the sight from the weeping wounds was not pleasant.

None of the wizards had come out of their hiding place so she went up to Mitsy and braced herself. The dragon let out a muffled cry of pain as Saranon placed her hands near the slimy wet mess and healed the wound on her belly. While trying not to dry reach at the same time. Dragon blood stank, there were no two ways about it she went up and healed the dragon's face. Mitsy gave her a confused look as she tried to wash the smell out of her taste buds with her flask. There was a strange rustle from the other side of the river. Gabriel and the other wizards rushed out of the cave and jumped on their dragons. 'Quick!' Gabriel shouted.

Katholomu was ready before Saranon was and as soon as she had scrambled up he was off. The dragon needed no one to tell him it was time to get out. They flew hard back to Zaidek Keep, the dragons needed no enticement, their fear driving them back all the way. Katholomu hit the ground so hard his claws scraped along the stone paving. Mitsy misjudged and pelted into his behind. 'Whoa there, how many times have I told you to slow down?' Captain Graddon spoke to his niece.

Owen piped up, 'Mitsy was attacked.'

Captain Graddon went over to Mitsy, 'She looks pretty good to me.'

'That's because I healed her,' she spoke.

The Captain said in a serious tone, 'Yes I can see that, thank you.'

Saranon felt her cheeks heat up with embarrassment, and she took Katholomu back to his pen. The dragon was thirsty and the water splashed over the floor as he guzzled it down with a ferocious speed. 'Well, at least someone's happy,' she said as she left him in peace.

Her ears were still buzzing from the energy she had released. As she thought back it had been a lot of effort to fight only a dragon, but she did not remember seeing another sorcerer. The whole notion that she had missed that detail was irritating, and it showed on her face. 'Are you all right?' Mitch asked

She jumped as he scared her, 'Don't do that.'

'Do what?' He asked.

'Jump out. I'm fine, but Owen mentioned something about Dihan and I didn't see anyone.'

Mitch held back a serious laugh, 'You'll see them soon enough.'

'Thanks,' she was not looking forward to more evenings. The thought of hanging out with a bunch of smelly sweaty wizards did not appeal to her.

Perhaps Gabriel was right, she had not been using her sorcery much. The days were nice and warm as the Normisian summer brought out a vibrant heat. Pennie was waiting down stairs she could see her from outside her room.

When Pennie saw her, she asked 'How are you going with school?'

Saranon pulled a face, 'Riveting.'

'I'm glad to hear it,' her friend ignored her sarcasm. 'I see you've been letting your wizard run riot.'

'I wouldn't call Mitch a riot,' she commented.

'Suit yourself,' Pennie spoke with a hint of amusement.

If there was one thing she missed at lunch it was Mrs Harper's cooking. The food was fine, but it could do with something extra. Since Saranon's cooking skills were close to nil she was not about to complain. 'Now you see that lady over there,' Pennie pointed across the room. 'That's your competition she's been with your wizard.'

Saranon almost choked, coughing up part of her meal. Her friend looked triumphant, 'You're not jealous, are you?'

She cleared her throat, 'I didn't need to know that.'

She went over to get ready for training, as she walked out she had difficulty keeping a straight face. A couple of times she lost her concentration and Mitch gave her a nasty bruise each time. Afterward he came up to her, 'You seem out of sorts,' he commented.

'Have you been seeing someone?' She asked.

Mitch went silent for a moment and sat down, 'I've been seeing an old friend, her name's Alyssa.'

He could not look her in the eye so she spoke, 'I just don't want to find out through someone else.'

'Okay,' he replied.

It was not the best outcome Saranon was hoping for, but there was little she could do. Mitch had been an accident and she was going to have to live with it. Still she had not counted on it being so frustrating, if Pennie was gloating at her then others were sure to know. Yet she had already given him space and to take it back would make matters worse. She knew she would not be able to sleep as she stewed in her own thoughts. Without saying a word she slipped away into the depths of the Keep. The noises were comforting in the absence of people. Zaidek was content whirring away pretending not to notice her presence. She found a comfortable position lying on a soft stone bed as it melded to meet the contours of her form and she concentrated.

The sounds of everyday life were recorded in the walls of the Keep, to access them required silence. It was easier to focus on Mitch since they shared the bond. Through the Keep she saw glimpses of Alyssa, but that was not what caught her attention. She opened her eyes, the hour was late, she could sense the being. It had interrupted her thoughts, but how could she get to it? Even though the Keep was friendly there were some places it did not want her to reach. Whoever it was moved faster than she could. Saranon was wondering if she should give up when she caught a clear glimpse, it was all she needed.

CHAPTER EIGHTEEN

The calling of Zaidek

Saranon transported herself beside the Dihan and thrust her energy against the sorcerer. It only just touched him, but the effect it had on the wizards in the room was instant. Several of them jumped out of bed grabbing weapons, lunging at the sorcerer dragging him down. He pelted them off with ease, but the distraction was all she needed. She ran Tellembre through the sorcerer's back only just missing one of the wizards. He stayed there for a moment as she held onto the bond-breaker. The sorcerer let out a small effort before collapsing into a heap on the floor. The sweat on her forehead soaked down her chin, it was then that she realised she was in a male wizard dorm.

The thought left her as she cringed at Mitch's voice, 'What did you do? You can't come in here!'

Captain Mirshendy butted in, 'Now that's a bit harsh.'

The Captain was sweating just as much as Saranon and a few of the others collapsed with exhaustion. One of the wizards was wounded and taken away. The wizards were not as keen to remove the sorcerer's body. Captain Mirshendy spoke to her, 'So you finally found a Dihan.'

Saranon was in no mood for jokes.

Mitch was standing beside her, 'You shouldn't be here.'

'I'm not sorting out your problems too,' spoke the Captain.

She cringed in disgust, she glared at Mitch as the room cleared and spoke under her breath, 'Did you have to do that?'

'Did you have to show up here?' He retorted.

Captain Mirshendy spoke, 'Hey, are you two coming?'

It was more of an order than a question.

Saranon grumbled as she moved into the common area where it seemed everyone had gathered. Mitch like the others had managed to grab some clothes and find a place to get dressed. The commotion had woken some of the others. Gabriel, not wanting to miss out looked half asleep. 'What's happening?' Gabriel saw her, 'You're not supposed to be here.'

'Yes, we've established that,' Saranon replied.

The officers were getting ready to leave and Captain Mirshendy popped his head back around, 'Are you coming?'

It was more of a command and without hesitation she got up from the table. 'Wait, where are you going?' Gabriel did not want to be left out, but the Captain gave her a disapproving look and she stayed. 'Since you were so keen on starting this, you can help finish it.'

Captain Mirshendy led her out into the darkness of the non-habitable area of the Keep. Then he merged into the background leaving Saranon alone.

She was not impressed by the wizards approach to merging. It did not help that she had trouble detecting them, even though she knew they were there. Although merging was as much a part of sorcery, she had not grown up with it and the method still appeared out of reach. She grumbled to herself as she went along, if the wizards were going to be of little help, she was just going to have to find a way to manage.

She could sense several things going on in the background, but as much as she tried she could not get a grip. There was a muffled sound behind her, and a wizard appeared falling dead on the ground, this was not good. She glanced around; the environment did not suit her at all. She may as well not be here, she had been running around to no avail. Saranon could not see and felt completely useless. A boom ricocheted through the winding corridor and she felt the shock run through her skin. She ran toward it. A cascade of stallic energy exploded into the air sending hundreds of thousands of tiny particles flying. The energy lit up the space before being absorbed back into the walls of the Keep.

It was all she could do to keep away the feeling of fright. Saranon had been close to Keeps, but this was different. That type of energy was not meant to get this close to the inhabitants, or above ground. The stallic energy excited her senses as she tried to hold on, it was a feeble attempt as she felt herself let go to the Angeon. As her eyes opened, she could see the voids in the energy. The patches glared towards her, with hatred spilling over from the Keep wanting to be rid of the source. Saranon struck through the gloom and into the darkness. The Dihan fought back filling her body with pain, but this only made her more determined and she struck harder.

As the voids weakened she could feel the excitement of the Keep as it spoke to her, finish them. Before she realised she had done exactly what Zaidek wanted. Then she had wanted it too, as she stared down at the dust that was all that remained of the other Dihan. Captain Mirshendy was the first to walk up to her, his eyes showed his uncertainty of her, 'You did well.'

The words sounded sour in his mouth as he turned and left her alone. As she returned Gabriel grabbed her arm. Before she could think about what she had done, and dragged her deep into the wizard stronghold.

'You were awesome,' she whispered with excitement. 'Come and stay with us tonight?'

'No, I can't,' Saranon replied.

'It's all right,' Gabriel said.

'Gabriel we need to debrief, you can catch up later,' Captain Mirshendy was serious.

She did not feel like chatting, she was just about to say something when she felt her legs going numb from the floor up. She could taste vomit at the back of throat, but could not bring anything up. Mitch caught her as she fell,

'Are you okay?'

'No,' she replied.

The floor started spinning and she could hear the Captain shouting as Mitch rushed her to the medical area. Saranon could only just see the colours were a blur that plagued her mind and made her head ache. She felt Mitch's hand not wanting to let go and could sense his frustration of not being able to help. When she finally came too, Pennie was staring down at her, 'Can't you do anything normal?'

Her head was still spinning and she did not enjoy being greeted this way as her friend continued. 'You came into contact with stallic energy and you look like you only caught a tummy bug. Do you have any idea how weird that makes you?'

The conversation was not what she had expected, she was in no position to talk back and felt robbed of what she wanted to say. Pennie had changed and the world had turned upside down. She cried as Mitch watched over in silence. Saranon was no longer alone, but this was not how she had planned it. Her silent thoughts were broken by Mitch's soft voice, 'I think your friend is jealous.'

After a while she sat up. 'I'm done with playing the patient. It was nice, but this place is starting to give me the creeps.'

She walked with Mitch back to the wizard's quarters. She stood by the door, 'This is where I stop and let you go to your clan. What will you do when I find mine?'

'A whole clan of Saranon's, I don't think so,' he smiled.

'Yeah right,' she knew Mitch was kidding.

She did not see how her friend could be jealous. After all she was exiled and she could not stay in one place for too long without attracting attention or causing mayhem. Mitch and Katholomu were nice, but they tied her down. Being free to do what she wanted came with life's little catches. In class she stuck out for all the wrong reasons, there was so much she did not know. It hurt her to think about it all at once, it came crashing down around the insides of her stomach making her feel sick. How could her best friend be jealous of this? It did not make sense when her life was such a mess. The Keep grumbled back through the walls at her frustration as she beat her fist against it.

Pennie stopped talking to Jacob as she approached the pair. 'We are returning to Darkonia,' her friend stated in a matter of fact tone.

'Is that because of me?' She asked.

'Don't flatter yourself we have out stayed our welcome,' Pennie brushed a cold shoulder against her as she left.

Saranon looked at Jacob for solace, but found none. Her friend was doing the one thing she could not, return home.

As she turned away from Jacob she saw something move out of the corner of her eye, 'How long has it been Jacob?'

'What do you mean?' He asked.

'How long have you been bonded to Pennie?'

He stood silent for a moment before replying, 'Darkonia is a dangerous place.'

Then he followed after Pennie.

Saranon did everything she could to fight the urge to run after them. If Pennie did not want to be part of her life, her friend was doing a fine job at keeping pace. She hung her head with the realisation that she could not sort out Pennie's problems before dealing with her own. She hated feeling useless, it was like a bad dream happening all over again. The sky was turning black to suit her frame of mind, filling with a chaos of clouds settling in for the rain. It tempered along the walls of the Keep soon streaming down ancient paths and crisscrossing the grounds. The wizards had been irritable since the ambush at Furly's Gates and the mood had washed off on her.

She guessed that would be the end of it. Pennie would go back to Darkonia, and she would be stuck here. Gabriel who had been trying to get her attention for some time called out below, 'Saranon, there's someone here to see you.'

She was so struck by her own thoughts that she had failed to notice Rachel and rushed down to meet them. 'I hear you've been helping my fiancé Jerald,' Rachel spoke.

'Yes,' Saranon said as she realised Captain Mirshendy had forgotten to mention that detail. Then the Captain was like that.

'Ah you ready for the big raid?' Rachel asked.

Her expression said it all she hated being the last to know, 'What raid?'

'Zaidek's power is being siphoned off, I'm sorry I thought you knew,' Rachel replied.

That would explain the occasional interruptions. She assumed she had just been having trouble communicating with the Keep, but this was not the case. She crumpled her nose in disgust and then smoothed her expression again. It was not Rachel's fault and she had always been kind.

For a moment she forgot her troubles and embraced her friend's warm conversation. As Pennie commented, 'You've changed since I last saw you.'

'I doubt it,' she responded.

Saranon could not help but feel frustrated, everything seemed to be going pear shaped as she managed to say goodbye to Pennie. It was a warm embrace given by two friends that meant it. Then her friend put on a cold face as she went out to start the long journey home.

The clouds above remained silent and menacing with few gaps of the clear sky breaking through. It was an odd eerie feeling, as if the rain had stopped to let Pennie pass back through the mountains and on to Darkonia. The feeling of home panged at Saranon's heart, though she did not want to admit it. She was losing a dear friend all over again to a world she was fast leaving behind. She had the distinct feeling that were she to return to Darkonia today, it would not be the same place she had left behind.

Mitch broke his solemn silence, 'Are you sure Jacob is bonded to her?'

She turned to where she could no longer see Pennie. Then spoke, 'Yes, but then stranger things have happened.'

He shot her a look; it was not the first time he had appeared to read her thoughts. She almost felt relief when she could sense the strain of the Keep underneath her. How she had missed that, she had no idea. Yet knowing it was happening was not going to solve anything, which led to the next misunderstanding. Saranon had thought that the wizards were going to deal with the problem, but no, this was the domain of the sorcerers.

Thanks to her wonderful lessons she did not think her teacher Mr Oakliff would be recommending her for the raid. After all there were some fine students who excelled at making her look like an amateur. The four sorcerers had been acting rather pleased with themselves of late, which seemed to fit in well with what Gabriel had told her about the raid. Katholomu was purring as she brushed his soft undercoat. At least she felt she was doing something useful with her frustration.

'Do you need a hand?' Gabriel asked.

Saranon let out a sigh, 'Sure why not.'

'I heard you won't be going on the raid,' Gabriel commented.

Again she was the last to know, Gabriel saw the look on her face. 'I'm sorry.'

Saranon was not looking forward to missing out on the raid. Yet she was not going to complain as Katholomu rubbed his cheek against her.

'He likes you,' Gabriel said looking up at the dragon.

'I don't know what I've done to deserve it,' she patted the majestic beast before he curled up to sleep.

'Thanks for saving Mitsy,' Gabriel added.

'That's all right,' she replied.

It had been a terrible windy day that had broken into a storm. Just part of Saranon's schooling had ended as she heard it thundering down on the earth outside. The wizards were busier than usual, with the sorcerer population that had been growing at the Keep over the past few weeks. The sorcerers were now gearing up for whatever she had been left out of. In a way she was content to be left alone. She would have had several arguments by now, as it was she was having difficulty staying out of the way.

Unfortunately training with the wizards had not taken a break. She was busy glaring at Mitch, who was content taking his time. She could have sworn he did it on purpose. He moved her along, 'Come on.'

Even though Sienna was a sorceress she just seemed to fit right in, and no one batted an eyelid, if only it were that simple. Saranon followed Mitch down into the lower part of the Keep. They may not come across anyone, but the damage needed repairing and this was more of a fix it mission than anything else.

Before she knew it she had been roped into helping the wizards mend the large cabling. By using fields to hold back the Keeps energy while they worked. It was boring so she tried to lighten the mood, 'So I guess you're looking forward to things getting back to normal?'

Captain Mirshendy looked puzzled, 'Can you talk and hold that at the same time?'

Saranon jumped about, 'Yes, I can do this too.'

Mitch glared at her.

The time passed so slow at one stage she had resorted

to counting wizards, but Captain Mirshendy did not see the funny side. When it was time to pack up she turned to the Captain, 'Don't get me wrong, I like to help. Next time can you pre-warn me so I can bring a book or something?'

'That can be arranged,' the Captain said in a flat tone.

'I think we had better go,' Mitch manoeuvred her out of the Captain's sight.

Saranon whispered, 'What did I do?'

'It's what you didn't do,' he explained.

'Hey!' She exclaimed.

She was looking forward to a good night's sleep. By the sounds of it the wizards had managed to do enough work on the cables not to need her help again. She thought that was convenient. In some ways she did not envy her classmates. She had managed to make it through her first proper schooling. Even though she still had catching up to do her marks were okay. As her teacher had said she would still be able to catch up to the level where she was meant to be. That gave her some consolation, although she did not think that would ever help her fit in. Zaidek rumbled beneath her and Saranon felt queasy. She ignored it and went to sleep.

The next day felt strange only everyone else seemed not to notice. She went out to see Katholomu who looked as though he was more alert than usual, 'What are you waiting for?'

The dragon made a sound for her to listen and she stepped up against the beast. Even if she could not hear anything it was not polite to say so. Katholomu pointed with a small flex of his claw in the direction of the sound she could not hear. She gave the friendly giant a puzzled look, but kept on trying. She was straining to listen so hard that when the siren sounded behind her she jumped and almost tripped over his claw. He waited a moment before retracting it.

Gabriel was motioning for them both to go inside. Kat moved and took his time. The dragon still managed to beat Saranon, 'What's going on?'

'It's the Dihan,' Gabriel whispered as she stood beside her. 'They've found out about the raid we have to stay inside.'

'And wait?' She asked.

'I'm afraid so,' Gabriel replied.

Great, she thought, now everyone knows. She let out a deep sigh. For all the kafuffle, not much had changed within the Keep.

She felt like finding a quiet place to sulk, but Katholomu gave her a disapproving glare. Between Mitch and the dragon she was finding it difficult to have time on her own. As she moved into the depths of Zaidek she felt dizzy, her eyes steadied and she realised it was not her. The wind rushed over her head when the air sat still. A pull of energy tingled down her spine as her senses stirred on the edge of a heightened panic. Yet she remained still, her eyes wide waiting for the first sign of movement when there was none. Something strange was happening. Saranon rushed and looked outside to a glowing orange crimson sky. It was as though the sound had been sucked from the air and then the roar came enveloping her ears.

The blast pounded every step of the way, forming a mountain of ash. Sorcery whipped around with a fiery gaze as it seared across the open ground. Crackling with a violent force as it went, as though taunting her from a distance. Her eyes stayed transfixed on the smothering clouds rising to block out the last remnants of sky. It shaded the Keep with an unnatural darkness that echoed her thoughts. She watched on, mesmerised, as her senses tingled, awakening inside. The sorcery raged within wanting to be let out.

She found Gabriel cowering with several others and spoke into the noise, 'I have to go.'

Gabriel's tear filled eyes looked back at Saranon and she mouthed the words, I know. Saranon raced toward the stream of light, but her limbs were taking forever to catch up. She made out a black silhouette on the ground in front. She thought it was Katholomu, but when she looked up through the haze she realised it was something else. At first in the glow it looked like a zennigh, one of the large cats she had come to know from Darkonia. Something was different as she approached it, for in the eyes shone the soul of the Keep. She had glimpsed an ockren from afar, but had not dared to get this close to one.

She stood in awe as she hesitated without realising. The great beast stared unblinking with sharp yellow eyes. It pierced straight through her, with an unwavering gaze. The embodiment of the Keep could be a dangerous creature and she was standing beside it. She looked down and realised she was touching its short course fur. Its unsettling eyes stared at her as if in anticipation. She trembled, she had not seen anything like what was happening and it scared her. Usually Saranon's senses guided her, but now she felt as though she were on her own. That was what she had wanted since she arrived, though it frightened her in the unsteady gloom that covered the sky.

The irony of the situation bemused her as she clambered aboard the strange beast. Zaidek had not warmed to her, but necessity dictated otherwise. As she gripped the ockren's short mane she could feel the undercurrent of the Keep sweeping through her. It almost willed the Angeon to the surface. The energy welled in like a torrent taking over her senses. Guiding her with a renewed urgency as the voice of Zaidek filled her mind with an edge of desperation. The rough raging sky dug deep into the untamed ground highlighting the sorcerers' plight. Saranon could feel the Angeon showing, but her senses still gave her no direction.

It was difficult to tell who was friend or foe as she steadied herself on the ockren. It felt weird under her skin moving in a different way to a creature made of flesh and blood. She somehow felt betrayed as the glow became stronger. Sweeping back her hair in the unnatural squall and the roar passed behind her. The deadly silence surrounded her like a plague thickening the air and making it hard to breathe. The hot stale air filled her lungs with the smell of the wounded Keep. It caked her clothes giving them an uncomfortable damp sensation close to her skin.

Saranon caught sight of Bianca up ahead and then she was gone. The earth trembled beneath her with the pain of the Keep, and the ockren let out an uneasy roar. She drove the beast hard into the fray. A blast of sorcery hurled her to the ground and the great beast howled in pain. She realised she was hurt, but she was still nowhere near the breach. She had to summon all her strength to rise up and go on. She caught the glimpse of another blast out of the corner of her eye and answered it with the age old power of the Angeon. Her energy surged ahead cutting a wild path into the throng. Saranon could make out Caleb and some of his companions making their way forward. To think she was going to miss out on this, now that would have been too easy.

The great beast heaved forward in protest of what was being done, leaving her no time to think of what to do next. The Dihan attempted to block her way, making the journey slow. If she did not pick up pace she would not have enough strength left to carry on. The pain coursed through her, and she knew it was now or never. She summoned the great power from the deep, the power of the great Keep, Zaidek. She pulled it up to the surface with every essence of her being as the Angeon struggled within. It was not enough as she surged her energy downward with such force. Then before she had time to pull back the flow, the great surge from the deep filled her mind with all the anguish of the Keep.

She could feel the ground start to melt below her with the pressure. Trembling as it sent ripples creasing through the surface of Tordoren. The foul smell became stronger, burning as it passed up through the acrid air. For one brief moment she lost her grip on reality, and the molten dark sheal spewed up through the ground. Searing the earth as it went like an open scar, sealing off the edges of the Keep. The ockren raced, excited to be so close to the Keep. Saranon moved it toward Bianca who struggled to hold her ground up ahead. She and the ockren swooped, and Bianca jumped on as the beast held the Dihan in his teeth, then flung him into the sheal.

She could hear Bianca calling to her, but she was still lost in the power that coursed through her veins. In a mighty leap the ockren spun them away from the rising liquid. For the first time in the raging anguish that had taken over the Keep, Saranon knew what she had to do. She turned and let out the full might of her energy sending the sheal and all the energy of Zaidek back deep underneath the ground. The surge ran through her with a staggering might, taking every bit of strength with it as it left a hollow vacuum. Yet the flame of the Angeon held strong inside her. The energy of the Angeon ran deep as it melded with the Keep. The great arterial cable which ran underneath healed with such smoothness. It left no trace of damage except for the wreckage above.

CHAPTER NINETEEN

The raging heart from the deep

As the Angeon turned, the great echo of rage swept in a bright arch blasting across the plume of clouds, as the sparks fell through the air. The impact only just missed. It knocked her from the ockren, as she managed to hold fast against the lasting remnants as they whirled by. She held on through the surge fighting her way forward as the Dihan struck hard. The harsh ash hid their forms in the distance, with only just a shadow making each figure out up ahead. Saranon raised the energy with a wild surge, as her steady hands held strong. The full might of the deep power of the Angeon awakened within, calling to be heard. The blast held true as it made its mark, out into the cloudy depths hiding the path ahead.

The Angeon, filled with the last determined thoughts of the Keep. She held on with a stubborn resilience not wanting to lose ground as she stumbled. The dim chaos swallowed the first signs of the blasts as they broke through, burning at her ears as she tried to focus. Just for a moment a brief figure stood out of the clouds, the first glimpse of the sorcerer she had seen through the haze. She held onto the image as her energy rose. All she heard was her heartbeat thudding hard as she hurled the raging blast through the broken haze. The surge burned across the clouds of ash searing away the sorcery that lay thick in the air. As the veil lifted Saranon could make out the figures up ahead.

She caught a glimpse as they disappeared, vanishing before she could run after them. As she made one final attempt she could feel the last of the Angeon slip away under the surface, as a cold sweat covered her skin. She screamed in an anguished fit of frustration, as she half collapsed beating her fists on the ground. Tears ran down her face, but the Angeon would not rise, and she cried out. Her aching muscles filled the void as she gave out an anguished cry she was not willing to admit defeat. Yet all the strength of the Angeon had locked itself deep within, and she pounded the surface of Tordoren one last time with her fist.

The Keep lay calm beneath not uttering a word. As the sheal cooled with a strength that would hinder any further attempt to siphon its energy. Saranon felt numb inside, it was not the victory she had wanted, as the Keep simmered just below the surface. The hurt left over from the fight mirrored her thoughts as she tried to make sense of it, the Keep was not ready to let go. She took a deep breath and the last remnants of the haze filled her lungs. Behind her the ockren stood with Bianca still showing the wounds from her ordeal. She stood hesitating, before clambered atop the guardian of the Keep. As the ockren turned, she took one last glimpse behind her. The Keep was safe, yet the victory felt hollow as she let out a deep resounding sigh.

The ground trembled with the changes beneath it as the Keep renewed its strength. It still seethed underneath the surface. The heavy wounds showed like a scar across the landscape, stretching far along the scorched earth. The chaos and injured people filled her ears, as the sky stained with the hues of the fiery blasts faded. Saranon could see the other sorcerers around her taking charge. The wizards that had been so long silent rushed forward to help. It was easy for her to ignore the dangers, after all she was a sorceress, but the wizards would have fared worse. She let Bianca down into the arms of the waiting Palascene. As she slid off the ockren's back it disappeared into the depths of the Keep leaving her alone.

She glanced around this was not how she had wanted it to end. She held out her hands in awe at what she had done, yet it was not enough. It was not what she expected as a weary tiredness set in over her aching muscles. The Angeon had risen then disappeared and somehow she had to make sense of it all. She breathed a heavy sigh as she let go of the frustration from within.

Evan walked over with a heavy stride. Saranon thought he was about to tell her off for interfering. Instead he looked concerned, 'You are injured, go inside.'

She wanted to say something, but the words would not come out. For once she was out of breath, which was just as well because she wanted to give Evan an ear full. As soon as she stepped in the doorway Mitch ran to her side, 'Come this way.'

He cleared a path among the chaos to the medical area where Rachel greeted them.

After some serious words, and waiting long enough to irritate her, she asked, 'What's going on?'

'I don't think we can heal that, you will be left with a scar,' Rachel spoke.

Great, thought Saranon it can go with all her other ones, 'I can live with that.'

Mitch helped her lean back, 'I'll see you when you return.'

She held his hand, 'Thanks.'

Rachel did an excellent job as she peered down at her arm the scar was only just noticeable. Mitch strode up behind her, 'Thank you for looking after my home.'

'Do you mean that?' She asked.

'It is an honour to ride an ockren,' Mitch's eyes looked troubled.

It was written all over his face like it was the others. The wizards were in awe of her, and afraid at the same time.

'Captain Mirshendy needs someone to help repair the cables.'

'Oh, all right I get the hint,' she grumbled.

She felt like she had just been roped into the most

boring job in the Keep, as she sat in silence mulling over the past events. She thought the Captain would be happy, but for some reason the silence made him appear uneasy. He hesitated before he sat beside her, 'I know you don't like this work, but I appreciate it.'

'Couldn't you get someone else?' She asked.

'We all have to do our part,' the Captain spoke from experience as he moved away.

Saranon's arm hurt she stared down at the faint scar left behind and rubbed it. Just as she was feeling sorry for herself a great spark flashed across her vision and for a moment she was unable to see. She guided herself by her senses then the roar of chaos came and the screams hit her ears. For a moment she thought she had done something then she sensed someone running in the distance, as the Keep howled at the intrusion. She felt faint as she realised it was a distraction, someone was trying to get into the Keep. She was torn between helping the wizards and running down to the central core. Captain Mirshendy bellowed through his pain, 'Go!'

Saranon's body acted out of instinct, and her mind took a while to catch up as she took control. It was all too fast she could sense it, there were too many. For a moment she slowed down overwhelmed with what lay before her. She could think of no other way to save the Keep. The reality scared her, and for a brief moment she would have given anything to be normal. The Angeon crept to the surface as though summoned by the Keep. It leaked through her skin as the floor opened up creating a chasm which swallowed her whole. The energy of the Keep threw her down which such force that she only just managed to hang on.

The central core heaved as her body melded and Zaidek locked everyone else out. The impact was instant as it sent a staggering shock wave rumbling up through the Keep, the sound echoed above as it rang out. In the depths below the Angeon reached out, but the Keep had been tampered with, and she could feel her hopes sink. Zaidek was so sure of himself that she felt she owed it to the Keep to try. The great engine whirred around her. As she reached out to the intense chaos pounding through the whirlwind that lay deep within the core.

If Zaidek lost his grip, she did not want to think what would happen. The struggle raged along the outer walls of the central core. The energy of the Keep ran hot through her veins, making her weep. It had to be close, but she could not see it. The edges showed on the periphery, but when she tried to pinpoint it she grasped at nothing. The sickening feeling came down her arms, as the tension grew taking over the thoughts of the Keep. It had to be somewhere, but Saranon still could not grasp it. All the while her head thudded in the great centre of the Keep. For a moment she wondered if she was enough, the sensation was overwhelming and flooded her with tears. The Keep beckoned her on pulsing with the need for revenge.

She felt the queasy sensation of panic and her whole body felt like it was going to vomit. Then a glimmer made its way through the whirling flow and she saw it. With all she could give she strengthened herself and surged out her energy to cling on. The energy of the Angeon raged in the core, lashing out in the haze as it locked on in a violent struggle. Saranon managed to hold on only with the help of the Keep, as it focused with an intensity that frightened her. The hard shell of the central core creaked and groaned under the intense pressure. She held on as the dark energy gripping itself around the Keep, and it raged against the Angeon.

Zaidek grew wild with frustration lashing out at the dark energy with all his might. The intense ferocity overwhelmed her, heaving her into the full strength of the Keep. The raw stallic energy coursed through her for a brief moment, as Saranon lost control. The Keep drove her energy forward with the full strength of many years of experience. It blasted through the hard shell of the core and melting new conduits as it went. The energy raged within as the Keep drove on with a ferocity that brought her close to panic. The waves reverberated up into the Keep, and tingled along her spine as she clung on with all her might.

The Keep held onto the taint with an iron grip and brought it into the intense energy rising up from the core. The dying dark energy screamed in her ears, as it lashed out in pain and anger. The last remnant of the sorcery forged from the Dihan, loosened its hold. Leaving a hollow vacuum that enabled Zaidek to rush in with a renewed force. Sorrow filled Saranon's heart as the Keep continued without hesitation. It killed off the external energy source, as the taint would have done to the Keep. She wanted to leave, but she was stuck until Zaidek scourged the last remnants away. Her body was weary, yet her energy beat on around her at a solid pace. This was not what she wanted, but the Keep ignored her distress. It showed no mercy as it lashed out along the furthest reaches. She started trying to disconnect herself. She pulled away from the core and nothing happened. She gripped with all her strength, and with a great reluctance the Keep let go.

She struggled to clamber out with the energy buzzing below. Most of her strength was gone and she had to find more to lift herself back up towards the habitable area of the Keep. The struggle was immense, but she held on with the whirling torrents raging below. In the darkness the sweat made Saranon's hands slippery. The crashing around her made her think of the turmoil outside, but she had to go on. The loneliness crushed in upon her as she reached the outer layer and realised she had farther to go. The Angeon slipped away as she came back to reality and the pain set in. It was a terrible feeling running through her muscles, but she had to go on. The way ahead was dark and grubby, the air smelled like charred ash as it filled her lungs with every breath.

As she clambered along Saranon found a rope. She clung onto it, and was dragged to the surface with the soot breaking off over her clothes as she went. Mitch held out his hand and hauled her up into the light, 'I thought you'd never make it.'

The light stung her eyes as she spun around. Part of the outer areas of the Keep had gone to rubble, but the heart remained standing strong against the smouldering sky. She clung onto Mitch, out of breath and exhausted. The landscape changed forever in front of her, with the heat still rising in steamy gushes from the ground beneath.

The last echoes of chaos still rung in her ears, as the sound of the central core lingered on as a reminder of where she had been. She gazed around at the haphazard mess as the wizards around her worked their way through the rummage. The main building stood strong underneath, like an ominous ghost hidden behind layers of ash. Her heart thudded in her ears as she took a deep breath and her muscles ached all over as she faced the small group of wizards.

Saranon strode forward, 'What have I done?'

'This was not your doing,' Captain Graddon spoke with a firm voice. He kicked the rubble away from his feet. 'I think you've outgrown this place.' He spoke with serious tone, 'We can look after Zaidek.'

She knew he was right, but she did not want to admit it. Mitch had always known that they would not stay. Compared to what had happened she did not think the scar was that bad, besides it was a war wound she could be proud of. The place was still a mess, although she was no longer needed by the wizards. Inside the Keep they had a great deal of work ahead of them to completely secure the Keep.

The Captain had already gone leaving Saranon annoyed. She had been quite content trying to avoid the whole situation, even though so far it had gotten her nowhere. She grumbled as she made her way down to the dragons. Katholomu was already thumping his tail in anticipation, which annoyed her even more. 'I hear you're leaving?' Gabriel said almost out of breath from all the rushing around.

'Yes,' she answered.

'It's about time,' Gabriel remarked

'What?' Saranon spoke before she thought, but Gabriel only smiled in reply.

She tried to take her time, but Katholomu knew what she was up to, and kept on nudging her to hurry up. Angry stares did not work on the great dragon, he shrugged them off. 'Are you ready?' She cringed at hearing Mitch's voice.

The marmoz dragon seemed to ignore her awkwardness as she clambered on, he was too busy scratching himself. Saranon sighed; they suited each other well. The morning brought with it a friendly heat that warmed the edge of the dragon's coat, making him glisten in the early sunlight.

Then she cringed as the dragon's claws scraped along the stone with a screeching sound painful to the ears. The noise was followed by a heavy thud as the dragon came to a halt. She opened her eyes; it was not the worst she had seen. It was enough to get disapproving stares from the others who were already making their way outside. To Saranon's surprise she saw Captain Mirshendy walk towards her as he came to see them off. The Captain waved as he spoke a short goodbye and she waved in return.

She laughed, she had come a long way, and could never have imagined herself in Normisia. The thought filled her with a great sense of pride, as Katholomu leaped into the sky with all the conviction of grandness. Mitch sat behind her, an odd companion, but welcome even so. The warm soft breeze blew in her hair as she clung onto the dragon's shoulder. Saranon smiled, she was free. A feeling she had wanted for so long.

ACKNOWLEDGEMENTS

Life has been a journey filled with many challenges, and the people I would like to thank would not fit on this page. To everyone out there who has been part of this incredible journey thank you, your support has been appreciated.

– Please Leave a Review –

For all the wonderful people who have read the book it would be fantastic if you can leave a review, this helps other readers find it. Thank you.

BOOKS

The Legacy of Zyanthia series:
Made in the Image of the Goddess
Running through the Rising Tide
Deep in the Shadow of the Fallen

AUTHOR

If you love fantasy with adventure and a hint of the unexpected the quest is about to begin. Escape into fantasy, and the mystical world of magic mixed with adventure. You are in good company although chose your company wisely. There are anti-heroes, wizards, and a range of chaotic characters ahead. Not to mention dragons. A fantasy world set in an ancient mythical world has to have dragons. Tales of sword and sorcery captivated Chantelle from a young age. Reading until all hours of the night to find out what would happen to the characters. There was just one problem the story would finish far too soon.

Hidden away in the distant past the life of a fantasy writer began. The real life struggles have been a saga all of their own for author Chantelle Griffin. Originally known as Chantelle Lowe and born in Tasmania, Australia. Her dreams haunted her from an early age. Vivid tumultuous dreams carrying adventure and danger. It took the author into a fantasy world filled with sorcery and treachery. The story continues to captivate her writing. If you love fantasy with adventure follow the Legacy of Zyanthia series.

www.chantellegriffin.com

GLOSSARY

ANGEON: 'The Angeon is Darkonia's answer to the Oracle, a sorcerer born with the ability to break down all defences and render a civilisation powerless.' There had been no Angeon since shortly after the Dreshan Occupation ended over 200 years ago with Zeralden Hadenvar the last Angeon who ruled Darkonia (as Queen) by marriage to the King's second son.

BOND-BREAKER: A weapon made by sorcery when dormant resembles a dagger, when activated resembles a sword it acts as a catalyst to magnify and aim the user's energy and can be used equally well by wizards as well as sorcerers. 'The most feared swords a sorcerer could use made of heart stone a melding of the elements to form a solid material that resembled crystal and sharp enough to cut through stone.'

CENTRAL CORE: The working core mechanism which powers the Keep, usually hidden away deep within the earth. It is a large engine created by sorcery which then continues to thrive on a combination of energy drawn from deep within the earth and sorcery. The combination creates a very raw and powerful energy which is difficult to manipulate.

DEAD ZONE: This is created when part of the Keep is not receiving energy from the central core or when energy has been diverted.

END NODE: Last outpost of a Keep's main energy source located at semi-regular intervals around the perimeter.

FERMADICIDE: Dark skeletal creatures.

FIRE MARK: A mark on the right shoulder to, the symbol of the fires of chaos given to the Issola in the camps.

HILAZEN: Bonded wizard.

HOST: Wizard joined with a Keep, it takes 60 hours to complete a union.

HYRIK: Restraint on sorcery, like a collar.

IMBENIK CHAMBER: Near the central core within the Keep, in between the indolin chamber and the central core it contains alters where a sorcerer can meld with the Keep.

INDOLIN CHAMBER: Inside the Keep, in between the habitable area and the central core.

KEDRIL(S): Tools to fix a Keep.

KEEP: A building protected by a central core powered by sorcery and energy from the earth. The tunnels led down to the primary systems and the central core that transferred energy from far below the ground into the core and turned into a usable energy source. Most central cores were located deep in the ground where the temperature was constantly warm…'

KULTIER: Long giant cockroaches.

LAY-LINE: Fast method of travel.

MAZETTE: Small (bird size) dragons.

MISQUEW: Riding cat.

NEFRELLE: Small creature (cat size), part human with very sharp teeth and claws.

OCKREN: Big cat, the soul of the Keep.

PALAFON: Tiny dragon.

QUADMAR: Aquatic creature from the murky depths, larger than a mermaid.

SACRA SEAL: Small, can hold it on your hand.

SHEAL: Liquid inside the Keep, very potent compressed raw energy.

SKADA: Small mechanical creatures that help maintain the Keep, they resemble a large spider.

SOVA BAG: A deceptive small light pouch that can become an enormous bag and hold a lot of objects, it will not hold living things.

STALLIC ENERGY: Energy from the Keep.

TALIK: Communication device. 'The sorceress held up her talik a small round disc that could open small enough to fit in the palm of her hand and placed her thumb on the centre of the outside…'

TRIDEN: Giant crab/spider, dark brown.

UVALEN CODE: '…A complex masterpiece describing the natural laws that governed sorcery.'

ZENNIGH: A large cat that normally lives within a Keep, they are too big to fit in a house but that has not stopped the occasional one from trying and getting their head jammed in the doorway.

ZYANTHIAN REGION: Armedicia, Taria, Normisia, Darkonia and Alveron were formed from one country called Zyanthia.